The Shadow Killers

Frank suddenly found himself face to face with a large, black-clad figure. The guy was dressed like a Japanese assassin, complete with black face mask.

The guy tried a ram's-head punch, and Frank reacted instinctively, blocking with his forearm and delivering a fast kick. Whirling swiftly, Frank delivered a jab with his right fist. His attacker, caught by surprise, took the blow.

But before Frank could press his advantage, he saw another moving shadow in the darkened dojo. Now it was two against one, and Frank went down.

As his consciousness ebbed Frank realized he was fighting real ninjas—Shadow Killers.

The Hardy Boys Mystery Stories

#59   Night of the Werewolf
#60   Mystery of the Samurai Sword
#61   The Pentagon Spy
#62   The Apeman's Secret
#63   The Mummy Case
#64   Mystery of Smugglers Cove
#65   The Stone Idol
#66   The Vanishing Thieves
#67   The Outlaw's Silver
#68   Deadly Chase
#69   The Four-headed Dragon
#70   The Infinity Clue
#71   Track of the Zombie
#72   The Voodoo Plot
#73   The Billion Dollar Ransom
#74   Tic-Tac-Terror
#75   Trapped at Sea
#76   Game Plan for Disaster
#77   The Crimson Flame
#78   Cave-in!
#79   Sky Sabotage
#80   The Roaring River Mystery
#81   The Demon's Den
#82   The Blackwing Puzzle
#83   The Swamp Monster
#84   Revenge of the Desert Phantom

#85   The Skyfire Puzzle
#86   The Mystery of the Silver Star
#87   Program for Destruction
#88   Tricky Business
#89   The Sky Blue Frame
#90   Danger on the Diamond
#91   Shield of Fear
#92   The Shadow Killers
#93   The Serpent's Tooth Mystery
#94   Breakdown in Axeblade
#95   Danger on the Air
#96   Wipeout
#97   Cast of Criminals
#98   Spark of Suspicion
#99   Dungeon of Doom
#100   The Secret of the Island Treasure
#101   The Money Hunt
#102   Terminal Shock
#103   The Million-Dollar Nightmare
#104   Tricks of the Trade
#105   The Smoke Screen Mystery
#106   Attack of the Video Villains
#107   Panic on Gull Island
#108   Fear on Wheels
#109   The Prime-Time Crime
#110   The Secret of Sigma Seven

Available from MINSTREL Books

THE HARDY BOYS® MYSTERY STORIES

92

THE SHADOW KILLERS

FRANKLIN W. DIXON

A MINSTREL® BOOK

PUBLISHED BY POCKET BOOKS

New York   London   Toronto   Sydney   Tokyo   Singapore

A MINSTREL PAPERBACK *ORIGINAL*

 A Minstrel Book published by
POCKET BOOKS, a division of Simon & Schuster Inc.
1230 Avenue of the Americas, New York, N.Y. 10020

ISBN: 0-671-66309-7

First Minstrel Books printing September, 1988

10 9 8 7 6 5 4 3

Contents

1.	Break-in at the Dojo	1
2.	Warned!	12
3.	Evidence?	19
4.	Black Death	33
5.	As Dangerous as It Gets	42
6.	Target Practice	52
7.	Department of Dirty Tricks	59
8.	No More Mr. Nice Guy	68
9.	Business as Usual?	75
10.	On the Road Again	84
11.	Too Close for Comfort	95
12.	Adding Things Up	100
13.	Stakeout	107
14.	Without a Trace	113
15.	"In This Corner . . ."	124
16.	Back to the Warehouse	130
17.	Yakuza!	139
18.	The Finals	147

1 Break-in at the Dojo

"Hieee-ya!" Frank Hardy gave a bloodcurdling shout, his hand flashing in a swift karate chop. His opponent twisted aside, sending a fist toward the side of Frank's head. Frank blocked and counterpunched in a blur of moves, never quite able to land a decisive blow.

"Hiieee-YA!" Frank's opponent snapped a quick kick, aiming for Frank's chin. Frank managed to block with his right forcarm. His loose-fitting white cotton suit was soaked with sweat. The guy circling opposite him wore an identical outfit, except it hardly seemed mussed, and the belt around his waist was brown instead of green.

The combatants' bare feet made squeaking sounds on the hard rubber mat that lined the floor as they both jumped to the attack. Frank found himself panting as his hands sliced through the air with knifelike motions. He whirled and

1

kicked with lightning speed. Yet his opponent was never there, twisting and blocking.

Finally, Frank moved an instant too slowly. His opponent slipped through Frank's guard, the heel of his right hand flashing out to stop an inch short of Frank's jaw. Frank raised his hand. In a real fight, that blow would have knocked him unconscious. "You win, Paul," he said.

Paul Pierson's face went from a mask of grim concentration to a grin. "Good match," he told Frank as they rejoined the line of karate students squatting on the floor.

"Yes, Paul, it was good." Their trainer, Mr. Watanabe, stepped in front of the line, his thin, intense face unsmiling as he looked down at his star pupil. "But we still need to work on the kicks. When you go up against Keith Owen next week, he is not going to show you mercy. At all. Am I right, class?"

"Yes, sensei!" came the shouted response from the assembled students.

"Up now for the final exercises. Up!" barked the karate master.

With an audible groan, the students rose from the floor and arranged themselves in precise lines on the hard linoleum floor, all facing Mr. Watanabe. Frank glanced over at Paul, who ran a hand through his sandy-brown hair before assuming his position.

Frank's own dark hair was plastered back with sweat. The muscles in his lean frame protested at the prospect of one of Mr. Watanabe's killer workouts. Frank wondered if Paul had the same problems. They were the same age, both seniors at Bayport High, both in the same physical shape.

But Paul Pierson was the class champion, a brown belt, just one notch below the coveted black belt. In five days Paul would go to nearby Riverton to represent Bayport in the regional karate semifinals; his toughest opponent was likely to be Keith Owen, the skilled but unpopular champion from a nearby town.

Frank frowned as he got into position. Keith boasted of his "killer instincts" on the practice mat. In competitions where the contestants were supposed to pull their punches, Keith sometimes hit at full strength. In the previous year's regionals, he'd actually knocked a kid out—an "accident" that had a lot of people rooting for his downfall this year.

Well, Paul Pierson was the one to do it, Frank thought. He even looked as though he enjoyed the torturous exercises Mr. Watanabe put them through.

Frank enjoyed karate, but the workouts were a bit much. He respected the discipline required, but Mr. Watanabe was totally dedicated about karate and expected the same kind of devotion from his students. The hard work had been well worth the effort; in the short time since Paul had convinced him to start classes, Frank had earned his green belt.

3

Karate training had been pretty handy in the real world, too. Frank and his younger brother, Joe, had faced lots of dangerous situations in the course of solving mysteries. It came with the territory—their father, Fenton Hardy, was a famous detective.

For about ten minutes the class performed the final exercises. Frank puffed his way through a punishing set of push-ups, which the students did on the knuckles of their clenched fists. They counted out loud with the sensei: *"Ichi! Ni! San! Chi!"* Frank tried hard not to think about the effort. Everyone groaned as they finished the last thirty push-ups and moved on to the equally grueling sit-ups and deep-knee bends.

Finally, the class came to an end, with a ritual Mr. Watanabe always insisted on. The students rose to repeat in unison their oath of respect for their sensei and the honor of the art of karate. Frank had felt a little funny at first, bowing to the slender, proud man. But he'd learned a lot from his sensei—Mr. Watanabe was worthy of respect.

Mr. Watanabe, in his turn, pledged respect to the faraway man who had been *his* sensei, twenty-five years ago, in Tokyo. Then he turned to face the class, and for the first time in an hour he smiled.

"Well done, girls and boys. I will see you next week. Get home safely."

He headed down the hallway, and the neat lines broke into a crowd of kids. They followed their sensei out of the dojo's training area and down the short hallway to the locker rooms to change. Frank stuck his head in the doorway of Mr. Watanabe's office.

"Excuse me, sensei," he said, knocking gently on the door. The karate teacher appeared lost in thought, staring down at his desktop, seemingly transfixed by the paper there. Frank cleared his throat, and Mr. Watanabe looked up with a start.

"Sorry to bother you. I just wanted to ask if you need help getting things over to Riverton for the match on Friday. Joe and I have a van, if you need us to bring anything."

"Thank you, Frank," said the sensei. "That's a very nice offer, but I think my station wagon will hold everything. Just bring a cheering section for Paul." Mr. Watanabe tried to smile, but his eyes went back to the paper and a small frown creased his face.

"Will do," Frank promised. "See you Friday." He headed for the locker room, where Paul Pierson and a couple of other students from the karate class were changing into their jeans and discussing the upcoming match. "I hope you really cream Keith Owen," one of the guys told Paul.

"If there's any guy who really deserves it, it's Keith," Billy Brown said.

"That's true," Paul admitted. "But I don't think he's going to be a pushover."

"Come on, Paul," Frank said, shrugging out of

his gi jacket. "Don't you want to win that trip to Japan?"

This year's regionals wouldn't be just any contest. It was part of a promotional effort by a large Japanese corporation, Oteman, Inc. The company president, Hiro Tanaka, was one of the biggest names in Japanese business. Amid much fanfare, his company was sponsoring this series of regional karate matches, with the champions of each match being offered a demonstration tour of Tokyo and Kyoto. It was expensive for Oteman but exciting for all the participants.

"It would be pretty cool." Although Paul was making an effort not to show his excitement, Frank could tell his friend was thrilled to be competing.

"So—pack your bags," Frank said with a grin. "Even if Keith Owen lets out all the stops in the finals, you'll beat him. No problem."

"I hope so." Paul grinned back. "It'll be some match." He shook his head. "If I hadn't been out with that sprain last spring, I would have my black belt by now. I may just beat Keith—in a fair fight."

Frank nodded. A lot of people complained that Keith Owen did more than take advantage of the rules—some even said he cheated. "The referees will be watching the championships like hawks," he said. "I don't see how Keith could try anything."

"In that case, I'll take Keith. And then . . ." Paul stretched out his arms like wings and made a

6

sound like a jetliner taking off. "Fasten your seat belts, puh-lease!"

"Think you could ever learn to eat raw fish?" asked Frank, slipping a T-shirt over his head. "Mr. Watanabe's always talking about sushi."

"To eat it—yes. To *enjoy* it? *Very* doubtful." Paul shook his head and began laughing.

"I'm sure you'll be able to find cheeseburgers over there," replied Frank. "Hunt 'em down, Mr. Tourist. You'll find them."

"And all I have to do is beat Keith Owen," mused Paul as he hung up his gi. He leaned down to tie his shoes. "I know my skills are better than his—I practice more than he does. But there's his—"

"Killer instinct," Frank finished for him. "Let's call it by its real name—he fights dirty."

"That's the word," one guy said. "Look at the way Keith clipped that kid last year. He nearly got tossed out for unsportsmanlike conduct."

"He's a bad loser and an even worse winner," said Paul. "He could teach 'Introduction to Gloating' at Bad Sports University. Well, I don't care if he's a crybaby. If he tries anything illegal, I'll complain."

"You won't have to complain," put in Billy Brown. A junior at Bayport High, Billy aimed to become a sportscaster and producer someday. "If Keith gets out of line, the judges will blow him away. After last year, they're really serious."

"This means war!" Paul said dramatically. Then he grinned. "Hey—maybe the judges are the ones who broke into that armory last night. Maybe they think they need some extra firepower to deal with Keith."

"Another armory got robbed?" Billy said. "Where was it this time?"

"In Kingsbury," Paul responded. "They got lots of guns and ammunition. Whoever is behind this acts as if there's *going* to be a war."

"Yeah. Hey, Frank," said Billy, "why don't you and Joe see if you can nail the guys?"

"Sure—we'll take care of it next time we get to Kingsbury," said Frank. In fact, the boys' father, Fenton Hardy, had been hired by the army and the FBI as a consultant on the case. But Frank knew better than to talk about his father's work, even to his schoolmates.

"It's some case," Billy went on. "Six National Guard armories robbed over the last six months, and nobody seems to be able to find a trace of the robbers."

"What's weird," Frank said, "is the way these guys can come and go without leaving a single clue."

"Come on, wouldn't you like to crack it?" asked Billy.

"I may be facing a case of attempted murder if I stay around here," Frank said, hurrying into the rest of his clothes. "Joe and Chet were going for pizza, and I'm supposed to meet them out front when they're done."

"You'll be the one waiting, not Joe. Chet can eat all night—especially pizza." Paul laughed.

Chet Morton was notorious in Bayport for being able to outeat any boy his age—which was saying a lot.

The boys headed out of the locker room, turning off the lights as they went. The main part of the dojo was in darkness, but a light still burned in Mr. Watanabe's office.

"'Night, sensei!" called Paul.

"'Night, champ!" came the cheerful reply.

Frank turned to Paul. "You know, I think there's something on the sensei's mind," he said.

"What do you mean?" asked Paul.

"I don't really know. It's just that when I talked to him earlier he seemed kind of distracted, worried even."

"He's probably worried about losing face with Keith Owen's coach over in Burnham," Billy said. "Heavy-duty sensei stuff—they're old rivals."

"That would be important to Mr. Watanabe," Frank agreed. "Maybe it would make him edgy."

"Come on, Billy," said Paul. "I'll give you a lift home. See you, Frank." They stepped out the front door of the dojo and into the night air.

"Yeah—see you." Frank leaned up against the low stone wall outside the dojo to wait for his brother, watching as Paul and Billy headed across the parking lot to Paul's beat-up old sedan. Frank knew it had been a sixteenth-birthday present from Paul's parents. It wasn't much to look at, but, as Paul often said, wheels were wheels. Paul had no complaints.

Frank waved goodbye, then found himself thinking again about the upcoming karate match. It would be a big thing for Mr. Watanabe—and Paul. Too bad their big competition had to be Killer Keith. That guy was into karate for all the wrong reasons.

Frank looked up and down the street—no Joe. He decided to go back into the dojo and talk with Mr. Watanabe.

As Frank opened the door, he saw the back of a brawny figure outlined in the light from the sensei's office. That wasn't Mr. Watanabe—so who was in the dojo? The figure was dressed all in black, not everyday street clothing.

As Frank stepped forward, he heard Mr. Watanabe exclaim something in Japanese. Frank didn't understand the words, but he caught the tone: surprise and fear! That was strange, coming from a twelfth-degree black belt.

The stranger replied rapidly in Japanese, unmistakable menace in his voice. Was Mr. Watanabe being threatened? If only Frank could understand what they were saying!

There was the sound of a car from the parking lot outside. Frank hoped it was Joe and that the two of them would be able to help Mr. Watanabe if he was in a jam with the stranger. But as Frank turned back to the door, he found himself face-to-face with the large, black-clad figure. It was like something out of a Saturday-afternoon movie. The guy was dressed like a Japanese assassin—a ninja—complete with black face mask. Frank would have laughed if the figure hadn't leaped to the attack.

The guy tried a ram's-head punch, and Frank reacted instinctively, blocking with his forearm and delivering a fast kick. Whirling swiftly, Frank maneuvered to deliver a jab with his right fist. His attacker, caught by surprise, took the blow.

But before Frank could press his advantage, he realized there was another moving shadow in the darkened dojo. Now it was two against one, and Frank went down in a rain of blows.

For the second time that night, Frank tasted defeat. Frank took a blow in the side of the head. As his consciousness ebbed he realized he was fighting real ninjas—Shadow Killers, trained to kill.

2 Warned!

"Frank!"

Hearing his name forced Frank Hardy to open an eye. He was still in darkness, with a husky form leaning over him. For a confused second, he thought he still faced the ninja, then he caught a glint of blond hair—it was his brother, Joe.

"Are they still here?" he asked, fumbling to get up.

"Those two guys? They were beating it out the side door when I came in. I started to follow and tripped over you."

Frank put a hand to his head, trying to stop the room from spinning. "Come on. I want to check Mr. Watanabe."

Frank was a little unsteady on his feet as he and Joe made their way to Mr. Watanabe's office. He felt worse when he looked inside, to find Mr. Watanabe sprawled behind his desk.

"He's still breathing," Frank said, dropping to

his knees. "Joe, call the police emergency number."

"Who'd do this?" Joe wondered as he dialed.

"Would you believe ninjas?" Frank said.

Joe stared at him. "We're in Bayport, not Tokyo. You'd—" He cut off as the phone was answered. "This is Joe Hardy," he said. "My brother and I are at the Bayport martial arts studio, and there's been some trouble here. It looks like Mr. Watanabe has been pretty badly hurt. Can you send some help at once? Good. Right. Thanks."

Joe turned to Frank, who had found a blanket and was wrapping it around the sensei's still form. "Now will you give me a straight answer, or have you been watching too many kung-fu movies?" he demanded.

"I saw a guy in a black ninja suit," Frank answered. "Who else could take out a twelfth-degree black belt?"

"What can those guys possibly want with the sensei? They must have him confused with somebody else."

"No, I don't think so," replied Frank. "Mr. Watanabe was arguing with one of them. Sounded as if he knew him. I only wish I could have understood what they were saying." Frank rubbed his throbbing head and winced. "A lot of help I was to poor Mr. Watanabe. I didn't even have a chance with those guys."

"Don't feel so bad—it was two against one. If it hadn't been for Chet's extra pizza, I would

13

have been here to even the odds." The younger Hardy grinned at his brother and sliced the air with an imitation karate chop.

Both boys turned to the door as they heard the approach of sirens splitting the peace of the summer night. In a few moments an ambulance had arrived bearing the emergency medical team. While two technicians crouched over Mr. Watanabe, another took a quick look at Frank.

"Didn't do yourself any good in here tonight, Frank. Still, you boys always seem to come out of these things in one piece. Your teacher didn't get off so easy. By the looks of him, I think he's lucky to be alive."

"Thanks for coming, Dave," said Frank. The EMT on duty, Dave Bateman, was a few years older than the Hardys and had met the young detectives at the scene of several emergencies.

"Who did this to him?" asked Bateman.

Frank hesitated. He knew he should answer Dave's question, but if Joe had problems believing him, he could imagine Dave's reaction. With the headache he had now, Frank was in no mood to be smiled at by his elders.

Joe sensed what was happening and stepped into the silence. "They jumped him in the dark. Two guys, I think. I was just pulling into the parking lot when I saw two men leave by the side door. I didn't realize that they had broken into the dojo until I found Frank and Mr. Watanabe out cold."

"Funny. There's not much worth stealing

14

around here—just some sweaty workout clothes," a voice said from the door.

The boys looked up to see Con Riley of the Bayport police standing in front of them, a squadcar light sending red flashes over his broad shoulders. "No reason to attack Frank or Mr. Watanabe, either. I'm interested in how someone could do this kind of damage to a karate expert," Con went on. "Looks like you've been tangling with some pretty mean characters."

He shook his head as Frank began to make his statement.

As Frank spoke, he kept sending anxious glances over his shoulder. The ambulance team had Mr. Watanabe on a stretcher now, and the sensei still had not regained consciousness. They left, and Frank forced himself back to the business at hand. There was little he could do for the sensei now, so he settled in to tell his story to the police.

Once he and Joe had finished their statement —leaving out their impression that the sensei's attackers had been ninjas—the boys headed for the van in the parking lot. As Joe started the engine, Frank popped a tape into the cassette player.

"This may have been a mistake," he said as a pounding bass beat came out of the van's speakers.

"Has your conk on the head changed your taste in music?" Joe asked with a smile.

"It just put me in the mood for something

15

quieter." He turned down the volume. Then, leaning back into the seat, he closed his eyes, and played chords on an imaginary guitar.

The boys came home to a still house. With Fenton Hardy working long hours on the armory robberies case, their mother and their aunt Gertrude had taken advantage of a friend's offer to borrow a resort condo for a few weeks.

"Awful quiet," Joe said as they sat at the kitchen table. "I never thought I'd miss Aunt Gertrude's voice."

"Right now, I miss her cooking," Frank admitted, building himself a tall ham and cheese sandwich as a belated dinner.

Joe had to smile. He'd been a little worried to find his brother kayoed on the floor. But the way Frank was attacking that sandwich told Joe that he didn't have to worry at all.

"What bothers me about this whole thing," Frank was saying between bites, "is that the sensei is such a quiet guy. He never seemed to have an enemy in the world—at least until this."

"From what you've told me about him," Joe said, "I'd have a hard time believing he'd ever had trouble with anybody. Maybe there's something in Mr. Watanabe's past—something that happened even before he came to Bayport."

"Whatever it is, it looks like more than an old

grudge," Frank said. "We should check it out—starting tomorrow. Right now, I've got the Headache That Destroyed Cleveland. The best place for me is bed. We can talk to Dad about this in the morning."

"Hey, come on," said Joe with a smile. "Don't you think that we should catch that karate flick on the late show? You could brush up on your footwork."

Frank gave his brother a playful jab in the shoulder. "Tomorrow," he said, heading up the stairs.

Tired as he was, Frank had a hard time sleeping. Every time he began to slip into unconsciousness, some warning sense pulled him back into a halfway state of sleepy awareness.

Finally, he squeezed his eyes shut, going through a series of relaxing exercises the sensei had taught him. At last he went floating off.

Sometime later, Frank found himself snapping awake again. It might have been the aftereffect of a crazy dream, but he had the feeling that something, or *someone*, was moving inside his bedroom. Squinting into the darkness, he couldn't see anything.

"Joe?" he asked softly. Frank wouldn't put it past his younger brother to pull some sort of prank on him. He started to sit up, and one of the shadows around the bed suddenly moved.

The cold edge of a knife blade pressed against Frank's throat. He froze in his awkward position.

A raspy, menacing voice whispered in his ear.

"You were wise enough not to mention us tonight," the Shadow Killer's voice hissed. "Be wise enough not to interfere any more—or your death will come fast and without warning."

3 Evidence?

Frank lay very still. He was completely awake now. Every muscle in his body was taut and ready for action, and the fog that had clouded his brain had disappeared. He felt the edge of the blade press deeper into his throat.

His mind raced, analyzing the situation. Clearly this visitor did not intend to kill him tonight. He could have done that easily. But the warning was clear. This guy meant business.

With his eyes adjusting to the dark, Frank took a look at the intruder. He saw the same anonymous figure, dressed in black from head to toe, with a black face mask hiding all but his eyes. If Frank saw the man on the street the next day, he would never be able to recognize him.

"You have heard my message," said the intruder. "Let us hope that you take it to heart."

For a second, the knife blade against Frank's

19

neck eased. This was his chance! With one swift motion Frank hurled himself out of bed.

The ninja moved even faster. With the grace of a leopard in the dark, the black-clad figure moved across the room, toward the window. Then he seemed to vanish.

Frank reached the window in two strides, peering outside. The midnight blackness showed nothing. The guy had melted away into the night, without a sound.

"I don't believe this!" Frank whispered to himself. This guy wasn't just frightening. His skill was unbelievable. Frank left his room, heading down the hall to Joe's. He opened the door and saw that his brother was fast asleep. Frank leaned across the younger Hardy and gave him a frustrated shake.

"You missed the fun, Sleeping Beauty," Frank whispered.

Joe was awake in an instant. He sat up and switched on his light. "What's going on?"

"I had a visitor. A salesman. He wanted to show me the latest in cutthroat knives. Slices, dices . . ."

"But you showed him the door, huh?" Joe gave his brother a grim smile.

"Not really," Frank admitted. "He didn't give me much of a chance. He left through the window."

Joe frowned. "Con Riley was right. These guys play pretty rough."

"But they're not playing smart," Frank said.

"It's like something has shaken them up. This guy gave away the fact that they knew what we'd told the cops." He frowned. "Or hadn't told them. So why would they bother to threaten us?"

"Maybe the mistake they made was Mr. Watanabe," Joe suggested. "If they were around to hear what we told the cops, they also saw Mr. Watanabe being taken away in the ambulance. Your sensei may be in a lot of danger."

"Con promised me he'd be guarded," Frank said. "We've definitely got a case, though. I want to give this our full-time attention until we get to the bottom of it."

"You've got it," said Joe. "I think we'd better let Dad know about it."

"We can fill him in tomorrow morning—or rather, this morning. Let's try to get some sleep with what's left of the night—we shouldn't be getting any more visitors."

Joe nodded. "Right—until they see us investigating."

Despite the adventures of the previous night, Frank and Joe were up early. They spent the best part of an hour searching the yard and the driveway for any clues that might have been left by Frank's midnight caller, but nothing turned up.

"Sure you didn't dream this guy?" Joe asked.

They headed back into the house, where their father was sitting at the breakfast table. "There are extra eggs on the stove," Fenton Hardy said,

21

shaking his head. "If I'm abandoned to make my own meals, I might as well cook for everyone." He looked at them keenly. "You're usually not up this early. Got a case?"

"Funny you should say that," Joe began as they joined him at the table.

"Not so funny," Fenton Hardy said. "You're up at the crack of dawn, and that didn't look like yard work you were doing out there. What's going on?"

Between bites of breakfast, Frank told him about the attack on Mr. Watanabe and the follow-up visit of the night before. Frank also told Joe and his father about his chat with Mr. Watanabe right after class—and how distracted the sensei had seemed.

"I knew something was worrying him," Frank said, frustrated. "So why wasn't I on my guard while I waited for Joe, instead of daydreaming?"

"You can't blame yourself for not being a mind reader," Fenton told him. "Mr. Watanabe obviously thought he could handle whatever the problem was."

Frank frowned. "Looks like he was wrong. But the real issue is—why attack the sensei?"

"I have to admit I'm surprised by the attack," Fenton Hardy told his sons. "To be honest, the whole idea of a ninja in Bayport is a little hard to believe. But the fact is, whoever broke into the dojo—and Frank's room—was very well trained. And with those black outfits and masks, either

22

we've got ninjas—or people acting like ninjas—operating around here."

"How is *your* case going, Dad?" Joe asked, changing the subject.

Fenton Hardy shrugged. "We have a task force of investigators—army intelligence, FBI, and local police detectives. Frankly, we've got more people working on those armory burglaries than we have leads."

He shook his head. "Usually, those weapons would go on the market in every big city—word gets out on the street, and we can get information from informers. But this time, nothing—the guns and the thieves just seem to disappear."

"None of the weapons have turned up?" asked Frank. "Somebody must be using them for *something*."

"Nope," said Fenton Hardy. "We expected the stolen weapons to turn up in the usual places—at the scenes of other, less spectacular crimes. But so far there's been absolutely nothing."

"How about your organized-crime informants?" asked Joe. "They should be able to give you a line on an operation this big."

"They're as baffled as we are," Fenton Hardy told him. "I'm beginning to believe that the usual organized-crime links aren't involved. This may be a completely independent operation."

"So why are they stockpiling the weapons, instead of selling them?" asked Joe.

"Exactly," replied his father, with a thoughtful

look in his eye. "They've got enough for a small army. That's what has us all so worried."

He rose from his chair. "But you have your own worries, boys. Are you going to stop by the hospital and see how Mr. Watanabe is?"

"That's our first stop, Dad," said Joe. He and Frank went to the door. "Good luck on your case."

"Not to mention washing the dishes," Fenton Hardy called after them as they headed for their van.

"As soon as we find out if the sensei is okay, I think we'd better have another look around the dojo," said Frank as he took the wheel.

"Right," said Joe, climbing in on the passenger side. "There must be something there to give us a line on this ninja connection."

"I'm going to swing past Paul's house after we hit the hospital," Frank said as he started the engine. "Mr. Watanabe gave him a set of keys so he could get in some extra practice before the big match."

Moments later, the boys had parked in the hospital parking lot and walked up to the information desk. The duty nurse, a tall, imposing woman in a spotless white uniform, looked up. "How can I help you?" she asked.

"We'd like to see Mr. Watanabe," Joe said.

That got him a headshake. "Visiting hours don't begin until this afternoon," the nurse said. "And Mr. Watanabe is in intensive care. Absolutely no visitors."

24

She glanced down the hallway toward the Intensive Care Unit, where a uniformed policeman stood guard at a door.

"Can you at least tell us how he's doing?" Frank asked.

The nurse punched a couple of buttons on a computer terminal and read a screen. "I'm afraid Mr. Watanabe's condition hasn't changed. He's still unconscious but stable." She frowned. "Prognosis: uncertain."

"I know he has no relatives here in Bayport," Frank said. "Is there anything we can do for him?" Concern for the sensei filled his voice.

"I wish there were," said the nurse. "But as I told the man who phoned this morning, there's really nothing anyone can do. The doctors and nurses here will give him the best care, but in these cases, a lot depends on the patient." Frank and Joe exchanged glances. Who had called inquiring after Mr. Watanabe's condition? And how had he known he was in the hospital?

"We've informed his relatives, of course," the nurse went on. "But until he's out of intensive care, we'll all just have to wait—and hope."

"Well, thank you anyway," Joe said, digging into his wallet to find one of his father's cards. "If you think of anything at all, be sure to give us a call at this number." He handed her the card, then he and Frank headed outside.

As soon as they were in the van, Joe asked, "Who do you think this morning's caller might be?"

"It could be someone like us, who wanted information on how the sensei was doing in intensive care." Frank's face was grim. "Or it could be the person who put him there in the first place."

Joe's face was just as serious as he nodded. "Well, if they come back to the hospital, they won't get too far. Con Riley has a watch on the door."

"And that's the only way into the Intensive Care Unit," Frank said. "No windows to sneak through. I think the sensei will be fairly safe right under the eyes of a duty nurse."

"I hope so"—Joe glanced over at his brother—"because we may be dealing with professional assassins here."

"And we don't even know why," Frank said, pounding the dashboard in frustration.

Joe put the van in gear, and they headed south to Paul's house to pick up the keys to the dojo. "Have you thought of what you're going to tell Paul?" Joe asked as they neared the house.

"I've thought—and I'm dreading it," Frank replied.

The Hardys turned into Paul's driveway. Their friend was in the front yard, mowing the lawn. When he saw the van swing into the driveway, he turned off the mower.

"Hey!" Paul greeted them enthusiastically. "You guys are just what I need—the perfect excuse to knock off mowing the lawn.

So tell me, has Bayport's detecting duo come to solve the mystery of the disappearing lemonade? This way to the kitchen to examine the evidence."

Joe and Frank looked solemn. "We've got some bad news, Paul," said Frank. He filled his friend in on the break-in at the dojo and the attack on Mr. Watanabe.

Paul's fists clenched around the lawn mower's handles as he listened to the news. "Ninjas?" he finally said, staring at Frank. "Are you sure? I mean, you were in a martial arts dojo, and this guy in black attacks you—"

"Wearing a black ninja mask," Frank finished for him. "We really want to get to the bottom of this, if we can."

"Of course," said Paul. "Do you think there's any way I can help?"

"For now, you can give us your keys to the dojo. And as the sensei's star pupil and unofficial second-in-command, you can give us permission to go look around."

"You've got it," agreed Paul. They headed into the house. The Hardys waited in the kitchen while Paul found the keys to the dojo.

"Here you go," said Paul. He gave them the keys and offered lemonade all around.

"I wouldn't mind a glass," said Joe. "Then we'd better get over there."

"What do you think this will mean for the match on Friday?" Frank asked.

"Ordinarily, I'd say it wouldn't affect it at all," said Paul. "But I have heard through the grapevine that Mr. Tanaka, the president of the company sponsoring the regionals, is very serious about the rules."

"And?" asked Joe.

"Well, one of the rules says that each competitor must be sponsored by a recognized sensei. With Mr. Watanabe in a coma, how can he be there?" Little worry lines appeared on Paul's face. "Poor Mr. Watanabe—he really wanted me to compete."

"There must be something we can do about getting you in," said Frank quickly. "Don't worry. We'll find a way. If I have to, I'll go talk to Mr. Tanaka myself. But I hope Mr. Watanabe will be well enough by Friday to send a substitute sensei, even if he can't come himself."

"We'd better get going," Joe said, finishing his lemonade. "Thanks for everything, Paul. Now you'd better get back to that lawn." He flashed Paul a grin. "Or your parents may tell you that the match is off—then you won't have Mr. Tanaka to blame."

"Okay." Paul managed a smile as he started the mower. "I'll try to solve my problems one at a time. So long, guys!" he shouted over the roar of the power engine.

The boys waved as they climbed in the van. It took only a few minutes to reach the dojo. They let themselves in and went down the hall. As they approached the main studio Frank suddenly froze. "We've had visitors," he said, staring at the pile of practice mats torn up from the floor.

"Doesn't look like a police search, does it?" Joe said as they headed back down the hallway to Mr. Watanabe's office. It was a small room, the walls covered in bamboo matting. Stepping in there had always felt like a visit to Japan. But now the office's Zen neatness was completely shattered.

The usually immaculate desk was strewn with papers, and the small pottery jar that decorated the desk was on its side, broken. "Samurai search party," Frank muttered, looking around. "Let's check the outside and see if they left any clues."

Once again, there was no trace of the attackers. Still, the boys made a search of the parking lot and the grassy areas surrounding the school. Then they turned their attention back to Mr. Watanabe's office.

"Boy, I never knew running a karate school could be so complicated," Joe said as he gathered up the files spread over the desk. "Look at all this paperwork. County health-code compliance, quarterly tax forms, incorporation papers—you name it."

"Yeah—the government uses lots of paper," his brother agreed. "But I was hoping we'd find something else." He opened and closed the drawers of the file cabinet. "Looks like every-thing in here wound up piled on the desk. Let's try the desk drawers."

Except for a list of the students, with names, addresses, and class rank, most of what they found were business letters. "You'd think Mr. Watanabe didn't have a private life," Frank said, setting another stack of papers aside.

"Maybe this will tell us more about him." Joe held up a desk calendar. "Looks like he jotted down all his appointments." Joe scowled. "In Japanese."

"Maybe we could get someone to translate for us," Frank suggested, but he still looked disap-pointed. If the ninjas had returned and searched the place, they probably had found what they were looking for already.

"One more place to look," said Frank as he got down on his knees under the sensei's desk. "Nothing on the bottom of the drawer. Joe, pull it out, will you?"

As Joe slid out the drawer Frank peered up. All he saw was the rough underside of the desktop. Then, with the drawer half out, a piece of paper appeared. No, an envelope, taped to the wood. Frank carefully pried it loose.

"What have you got?" Joe asked.

"I don't know, but Mr. Watanabe went to enough trouble to hide it."

Frank stood up, holding the envelope carefully by its edges, and laid it on top of the desk. He

30

opened a flap at the side and pulled out a piece of paper.

"Well, we're finally getting somewhere," Joe said.

"Maybe," Frank said, with a trace of disappointment in his voice. "But we're going to need help."

He spread out the sheet as Joe looked over his shoulder. One side of the paper was covered with several long columns of Japanese ideograms, with a bright red seal of some kind in the lower right-hand corner.

"Another clue we can't read," Joe complained.

"I'll bet it's important," Frank said. "Otherwise, why would the sensei have hidden it so carefully?"

"I wonder what it is." Joe stared down at the ideograms. "Maybe a letter—or some kind of official document, with that big seal."

Totally absorbed in his examination of the letter, he leaned forward, resting his hand on the desk. A faint whirring noise made him bring his head up and look toward the doorway. He caught a flash of metal, then something thunked into the desktop, right between the fingers of his left hand.

The quivering object was star-shaped, but each of its arms was deadly sharp. It was a *shuriken,* a Japanese throwing knife—and a prime ninja weapon.

Frank vaulted over the desk, heading for the

empty doorway. But another shuriken whizzed in, missing him by millimeters. Frank landed and froze in his tracks.

"Good." The voice of the person outside the door was soft, almost gentle. "Hold perfectly still. I'd hate having to nail you to that wall."

4 Black Death

A figure stepped into the doorway of the sensei's office. It wasn't the ninja they expected, although the girl who appeared was wearing black jeans and a black T-shirt. She was pretty, Japanese, and about the same age as the boys. Right now, her dark eyes were cold, and one hand stayed in the big leather bag slung over her shoulder.

"Okay, tell me who you are and what you're doing here," she demanded, "unless you want to test your reflexes." Her hand flicked out of the bag, another shuriken at the ready.

"Whoa, hold it," Frank said, his eyes on the deadly bit of metal. "My name is Frank Hardy. Mr. Watanabe is my karate teacher. My brother Joe and I are trying to find out why the sensei was attacked here last night."

The young woman relaxed, her hand slipping back into her bag. "The Hardy brothers?" she said. "I've heard about you—the famous detectives of Bayport. Okay, suppose you two give me a little information."

"We might just do that," replied Frank, "if you'll tell us who *you* are."

"Oh—sorry." The girl grinned at them. "I'm Tikko Shinsura. The sensei is my uncle. My family got a call about the attack from the police late last night, and we headed over the first thing this morning. My father is at the hospital, waiting for news of Uncle Seino's condition. I decided to look around here."

She shook her head. "It looks like a wrecking crew came through. Then I heard you two in here . . ." She stepped over to the desk, running a finger over the smashed pottery ornament. "My mother gave this to him," she said quietly.

"Tikko, I'm really sorry about your uncle," Frank said, picking up a chair from the floor.

"Me, too," Joe added.

"Both of us were here when the sensei was attacked," Frank went on. "Since then, we've been doing some investigating."

"I'd appreciate anything you could tell me," said Tikko.

"We don't have very much yet," said Joe. He leaned against the wall as Frank sat Tikko down in the chair and then seated himself on a corner of the sensei's desk. Quickly, the Hardys ran through the events of the night before. Frank didn't mention the midnight prowler, and Joe took the hint.

"One thing more," Frank said as he finished

34

the story. "The people in here last night wore ninja-style costumes."

Tikko glanced up at him, frowning in thought.

"Do you know anything that might help us?" asked Frank. "Anything at all?"

"It all seems so unbelievable," Tikko said. "Poor uncle. Lately he'd been acting sort of . . . different. So upset and nervous."

"What was on his mind?" asked Joe.

"I wish I knew for sure," the sensei's niece replied. "I only started noticing it after he sent us that package."

Frank suddenly sat up straight. "Package?" he said. "Tell us about it."

Tikko leaned back in her seat, looking from Frank to Joe. "We got it in the mail last week, but I think it's important for you to have a little background. Okay?"

"Absolutely," Joe replied.

"My father and I moved here from Japan right after my mother died, about eleven years ago. My mother was Uncle Scino's sister." She glanced at the shattered jar again. "My uncle came a year later. When I was a little girl in Tokyo, I didn't know my uncle very well. He was a very important man, though. Even more influential than my father, who was a big executive with an engineering firm."

"Was your uncle an executive, too?" asked Joe.

"Oh, no—he was a sensei. But that means a lot more in Japan than it does here."

Frank nodded. "You mean that karate is more

important in Japan, so your uncle was more respected."

"That's it. Here Uncle Seino is just a karate teacher. It's exotic, but not exactly serious business. In Japan, karate is special. It has long roots in our culture. And my uncle was one of the finest karate masters in the whole country—a legend in his time, a superstar."

Frank started pacing the small room. "So why would the sensei leave all that and come to the United States?"

"That's something I have never asked him," Tikko admitted. "Of course, the things that happened just before he left were reason enough."

"Tell us," Joe urged.

"Shortly before Uncle Seino joined us in Bayport, his house in Tokyo burnt. It was an old wooden house, very precious, and very beautiful. There were very few like it left—the city had grown so fast since the war. And the fire was so strange. My uncle's house was in the best neighborhood in the city—very carefully kept, lots of police and fire protection. Yet Uncle Seino's house burned to the ground."

"It begins to sound like arson," Frank said.

"I see why the Hardys are so highly regarded as detectives," said Tikko. "My father urged Uncle to go to the police. But Uncle Seino never did. In fact, he refused to talk about it."

Both Hardys eagerly stood over her now. There *was* something mysterious in Mr. Watanabe's past, but ten years had passed peacefully enough for the sensei. "So your uncle came to America," Frank pressed.

Tikko shrugged. "It seemed natural that Uncle Seino come here to join us. We just thought he was heartbroken over losing his home."

Frank nodded. "And nothing else happened— till lately?"

Tikko frowned up at him. "It seems all of a sudden, my uncle was . . . nervous. He visited us a short while ago, and when he got ready to leave, he did the oddest thing. He took a flashlight and checked out the backseat of his car before he got in."

Joe's eyebrows went up. "What was he looking for? A bomb?"

"Or *who* was he looking for?" Frank asked, thinking of the black-clad ninja who'd attacked him the night before. Those shuriken Tikko had thrown were ninja weapons, too. Maybe there was more of a connection than she was telling them. Frank wanted to know Tikko a little better before giving all their clues away.

"What about that package you mentioned?" Frank pressed on.

Tikko shook her head, looking troubled. "My dad and I were doing some yard work when the mailman arrived with a package addressed to my father from my uncle. We were both curious as my father unwrapped the brown paper. Inside was a box, wrapped in black silk, with some kind of Japanese symbol on it in red and white. I was really eager—I thought it was a present."

37

She looked more unhappy. "But my father acted as if someone had just handed him a poisonous snake. He didn't say a word—just went inside the house with the package. I haven't seen it since. We haven't even talked about it. I took my cue from the look on his face. I didn't mention the subject again."

"Are you sure the package came from your uncle?" Frank asked.

"Yes. There was a note enclosed. My father left it sitting on the kitchen table. Since I was curious, I read it."

"What did it say?" Joe asked, leaning forward eagerly.

"Uncle Seino asked my father to keep the box in a safe hiding place and tell nobody about it. The box wasn't to be opened unless my uncle died."

Frank and Joe looked at each other. That grim request made a lot more sense now. "Do you think you can find the box?" Frank asked. "It may be a clue to what's going on here."

"I don't think my father will tell me where he put it," Tikko said with a shrug. "But I guess I can search for it myself."

"Great!" Frank smiled. Finally, they were getting started. "Another thing I'd like to do is take a look around Mr. Watanabe's house. If we're lucky, something there might give us a line on what's going on." He glanced over at her. "Think you can get us in, Tikko?"

"Sure," the girl agreed readily. "I have a key,

and my father asked me to check on things there. It'll be nice to have company, too—now that I've heard about the attack on my uncle."

"You seem to be able to look after yourself pretty well," Joe said, pulling the shuriken from the wall behind the sensei's desk.

"I know a few tricks, anyway." Tikko grinned at him. "My dad taught me to throw."

After quietly pocketing the letter they'd found, along with the sensei's desk calendar, the Hardys led Tikko out to their van. The three climbed in, with Joe going into the back. They headed for the outskirts of Bayport, where Mr. Watanabe lived.

The sensei's house was at the top of a big hill, tucked away in a grove of tall spruce trees. The building itself was fairly small, two stories high, and made of plain shingles. Weathered wood glinted like silver against the evergreens.

"It's so beautiful here," Tikko said as Frank parked the van. "It reminds me of the countryside back in Japan. I think that's why Uncle Seino moved here—it reminded him of home."

"I wish I could visit Japan," Frank said. "Maybe Paul will take lots of pictures."

"Paul?" Tikko said with a questioning look.

As they headed for the door Frank and Joe quickly explained about Paul and the upcoming match, with the trip to Japan for the winner. They looked for any special reaction from Tikko, but she was only politely interested.

Tikko let them in with her key, but as she

pushed the front door open, the Hardys saw instantly that they weren't the first to pay a call here. Mr. Watanabe's house, like his office, had been brutally searched.

"I guess they didn't find what they wanted at the dojo," Frank said through tight lips. He and Joe surveyed the damage as Tikko stared around, dismayed.

"Poor Uncle Seino," she said as she took in the mess of the living room. She went to the mantelpiece and looked sadly at a scatter of broken ivory on the floor. She stooped to pick up the fragments and held them out to the Hardys.

"This was a beautiful samurai warrior, carved inside of an ivory ball," she said, "like a ship in a bottle, but more delicate. It was just about the only thing my uncle brought with him from Japan. He'd taken it in to a shop to be appraised on the day his house burned down." Tears began to fill her eyes. "It escaped the fire—only to have this happen."

The Hardys didn't know what to say. Joe just shook his head. "I'm sorry," Frank murmured as he helped Tikko gather up the pieces.

Joe headed for the French doors leading out to the garden. "This must be how they came in," he said, with a trace of anger in his voice. "I wonder why they bothered to use a door at all. Why not just blast through the wall?"

He squatted to take a closer look at the edge of the door, where a crowbar had been used to break the lock. Broken wood stuck out in jagged

40

points—and one of those splinters had snagged something.

Joe bent closer, carefully lifting off a scrap of black material about the size of a silver dollar with a spiral design embroidered in red and white.

"Take a look at this," Joe called. He held up his hand to show off the piece of silk. Tikko came rushing over.

"That's it!" she exclaimed. "That's the same symbol that was on Uncle Seino's package!"

"I've seen that sign before." Frank frowned, trying to remember. "It was in a book about international crime."

"International crime?" Tikko said in disbelief.

Frank's face grew even grimmer. "You might say it's a calling card. It's the sign of a particularly deadly branch of the ancient Japanese under-world—the Yakuza."

5 As Dangerous as It Gets

"That's impossible!" Tikko's voice went up in astonishment. "My uncle is a good person, not some crook."

"This says there's some connection between him and a Yakuza clan," Frank said, looking carefully at the scrap of cloth Joe held out.

"Do you believe my uncle would work for a bunch of gangsters?"

"I don't know what to believe," Frank said. "But it looks like somewhere, somehow, Mr. Watanabe crossed the Yakuza's path—and wound up with that box. Maybe he fought against them, and they finally tracked him down."

"I don't believe any of this," Tikko declared. "Yakuza, ninjas—it sounds to me like you've been reading too many karate comics."

"It makes a weird kind of sense," Joe said. "Gangsters might like to have people who can kill silently on the payroll."

42

"Sure—if you buy the ridiculous idea of ninjas hanging around a town like Bayport." Tikko obviously wasn't going to believe that.

"Well, let's look at our one fact," Frank said, holding up the scrap of silk. "The mark on that package the sensei sent your father was the same as this one—a Yakuza sign—and he wanted that package hidden. I'm not saying your uncle is a criminal, but it looks like the guys who came after him are."

Tikko stared at Frank for a long moment, then took a deep breath. "Sorry. If you're right about what the symbol means, we're up against something really serious—and dangerous!"

"Well, that's one mystery solved, anyway," Joe suggested. "Now we know why the sensei was upset the other night. Tangling with the Yakuza is no fun."

Tikko bit her lip, thinking hard. "My family never, ever discussed things like the Yakuza." A look of determination spread over her face. "If I'm going to help my uncle, I guess I'd better learn about the Japanese underworld. Okay, what can you guys tell me?" She sat down on the couch.

Frank shrugged. "The Yakuza are Japan's organized crime, like the Mob operates over here. But there's more ritual involved—the Yakuza is an ancient secret society. They're really into symbols of loyalty and power."

"Sounds like a college fraternity," Tikko tried to joke.

"With a big difference." Joe looked grim. "The Yakuza are ruthless killers. Money's not so important—except that it buys them power. If you offend the Yakuza, even without knowing it, you don't survive the mistake."

Tikko went pale. "That might explain what happened to my uncle, wouldn't it?"

"One thing about the Yakuza," said Frank. "They're easy to spot—they go in heavily for tattooing. Find somebody with a tattoo like this" —he pointed at the silk design—"and that'll be one of the guys behind all this."

Tikko took it all in. Then she asked, "So you think the men who attacked my uncle are part of this group?"

"Either they were members, or they were sent by the Yakuza," said Frank. "It's the only explanation for the sensei's fear—and that piece of cloth."

Joe headed out of the room. "I think we'd better have a look around to see if we can figure out what they wanted," he said.

The boys and Tikko began to search methodically. Tikko took the bedrooms upstairs, and the boys sifted through the wreckage on the first floor. After forty-five minutes, Joe was shaking his head. "Be nice if we knew what we were looking for," he complained.

"Hey, guys, take a look at this," Tikko called from the top of the stairs. In her hand was a manila folder.

She dashed down the stairs and opened the folder, revealing a bunch of newspaper clippings. Frank read, with Joe peering over his shoulder. " 'Japanese Company Sponsors All-Georgia Karate Championships,' " Frank read. " 'Oteman aids Massachusetts Martial-Arts League.' " He riffled through the others. "Delaware, Florida . . . these are from all over the East Coast."

"The dates begin a couple of months ago," Joe added.

"Sure. They're all about the karate meets set up by Oteman." Frank pointed to a photograph showing a smiling Hiro Tanaka, the president of the company. "It's probably just the sensei's way of keeping up with the really great karate students in the region."

"Well, Mr. Watanabe has his own star—Paul Pierson." He shook his head. "*If* he gets to compete, without the sensei."

"Maybe Uncle Seino will be better by then," said Tikko sadly.

"I hope you're right," Frank said. "It would be a shame for Paul to miss his big chance to go to Japan—not to mention his chance to cut Keith Owen down to size."

"Is this Keith a bad karate student?" Tikko asked.

"Keith's not bad at karate—just at following the rules," Joe told her. "Of course, if he starts playing dirty, you can always challenge him to a duel with shurikens."

Tikko laughed and, whipping a throwing knife from her bag, waved it in mock menace. "I just might do that," she said.

Frank grinned. The longer he knew Tikko, the more he liked her. He decided to let her in on the clue they'd found in the dojo. "Tikko," he asked, "how's your Japanese?"

"Rusty—but still okay," she answered. "Why?"

"Before you came bursting into Mr. Watanabe's office, we found this," he said, carefully unfolding the piece of paper they'd found taped underneath the sensei's desk. "I think it's important for us to find out what it means. Also, your uncle made a lot of notes on his calendar— in Japanese. I left it in the van."

"I'll be glad to help," Tikko said. "It's the least I can do."

"And let's not forget about that box," Joe added.

"Oh, I won't," Tikko said. "I can see it's important to find out what my uncle sent to my father."

"Good. Now I guess we'd better let somebody know about this break-in." Joe went to the phone and dialed the police. Frank kept scanning the wrecked living room, scowling in thought. His eyes came to rest on the jimmied French doors.

"Con Riley, please," Joe said. "Tell him the Hardys have another break-in to report."

Con was over in minutes. After filling him in, the Hardys and Tikko went on their way.

"Can you guys drop me back at the dojo?" Tikko asked. "I left my car there."

"Sure," Frank agreed. "But first a brief side trip." He stopped the van in front of a copy shop, taking the Japanese letter and Mr. Watanabe's desk calendar.

Moments later, he returned. "I copied this and the last few pages of the calendar—for insurance." Frank handed over the originals to Tikko. "Good luck with these."

They dropped Tikko off, and Joe looked at his watch. "Hey, we were supposed to meet Chet for dinner about fifteen minutes ago."

"That's one thing about Mom being away," Frank said. "We've seen the inside of every diner in Bayport."

Joe laughed. "And Chet's been loving every minute of it."

As they drove, Joe used the car phone to put in a call to the hospital. Mr. Watanabe's condition was unchanged.

"All of a sudden, I'm losing my appetite," Frank said. "I hope Tikko finds something in all that Japanese she'll have to translate. We really don't have much in the way of evidence." His voice was discouraged as he drove.

"Yeah. Mysterious, anonymous threats and a piece of black silk." Joe patted the pocket where he'd put the scrap of material. "Do you think we should ask Dad for some ideas?"

"Sure—the next time we bump into him." Frank grinned, but his smile faded. "Dad seems

47

to be working awfully hard on that armory case."

They pulled into the parking lot for the diner. "Right now, all I want to work on is a burger and fries," Joe said. "Come on. Last one in pays the check."

They hopped out of the van and reached the door in a dead heat. Inside, Chet Morton was hunched in a far booth, finishing off the last of a jumbo-sized soda.

"Well, it's about time the forces of law and order had time for their old pal," Chet said good-naturedly.

"Hey, Chet!" said Joe. "Feeling unloved?"

"Not anymore," said Chet, "but I'm curious about this case you're working on. I want the lowdown."

The three boys took a booth and ordered cheeseburgers.

"Come on," Chet challenged them. "I heard what happened to Mr. Watanabe. Don't tell me you're not trying to find who did it." He shook his head. "I'm sorry I didn't come along with Joe— we might have evened things up." Chet's stocky form carried a lot of muscle, and he had helped the Hardys in some rough moments.

"Thanks for the offer, Chet. But I'd have needed a lot more reinforcements to take care of those guys."

The cheeseburgers and fries arrived, and Frank filled Chet in on the case—but only up to a point. Chet could be a good listener, but Frank didn't want to make him a Yakuza target. After a rough thumbnail sketch, he switched the topic.

"What do you think of Paul's chances in the semifinals?" Frank asked.

"He's the best brown belt around—without a doubt," said Chet. "He'll go to the finals, no sweat. And then he can show Keith Owen how it's done. I just hope Paul won't choke without the sensei to boost him. Keith can be real nasty." He rested his forearms on the table. "But what can you expect from a guy with weird hobbies?"

"Like what?" Frank asked.

"He collects all those gross martial-arts weapons. I saw him once, showing off some kind of a knife with three blades. Not the kind of guy I'd like to hang around with," Chet said.

"What do you think, Keith's going to jump Paul in the ring with a samurai sword?" Joe laughed.

Frank didn't. "I'm more worried about after the match. If Paul beats Keith, that guy is sure to come after him. Bet on it."

The next morning, the boys were up early again. While Joe cleaned up after breakfast, Frank called the hospital to check on Mr. Watanabe.

"Still no change?" Joe asked, taking in the look on his brother's face. "Look. We're finished here. Let's go in and talk to Dad."

They walked into their father's study, where a grim-faced Fenton Hardy was reading reports about the armory case.

"This burglary in Kingsbury has been getting a lot of play in the newspapers," Frank said.

"Wait till they get the list of what was stolen," Fenton Hardy said, pointing to one sheet of paper. "The thieves got away with thousands of hand grenades and semiautomatic rifles—plus ammunition. They'd be better armed than most policemen trying to arrest them." Obviously, Fenton Hardy did not like the way the case was going. "What brings you in here?"

"The library, Dad. I want to look up some information on the Yakuza." Frank began leafing through reference books.

"First ninjas, now Yakuza?" Fenton Hardy said.

"Can you tell us anything about those guys?" Joe asked.

"I've heard of them, of course," the boys' father replied, "but I have never—as far as I know—had any direct experience with them. Not many people in this country have. Why don't you go to the *Bayport Times* and talk to Jim Lao? The Far East is his beat, and if anybody knows about the Yakuza, he will."

Frank put down the book he was leafing through. "Great idea, Dad," he said. "Let's go, Joe."

Heading downtown in the van, Frank glanced in the rearview mirror as he drove. "Looks like we may have company." He made two right turns, and a small gray hatchback behind them followed right along.

"Well, at least it's not a ninja," Joe said, staring into the mirror. "Just two guys in sunglasses."

Morning traffic still clogged the main roads, so Frank took a winding course through Bayport's back streets to lose his tail. They drove farther and farther toward the waterfront, until Joe finally said, "Hey, watch it! You don't want them to catch us against the bay."

"I know what I'm doing," Frank said, gunning the engine as they sped through a maze of old, narrow streets. He whipped around one corner, made a right, then a quick left, bouncing the car over a deeply rutted road behind a ramshackle warehouse.

He pulled up behind a garbage dumpster as their pursuers roared by the mouth of the alley.

"Pretty neat," Joe had to admit. Frank grinned and started the engine again.

But as he went to leave the alley, the gray car reappeared, burning rubber in reverse. It shot across, blocking the road, and the driver leaned out, hurling something at them.

For a brief second, they could see his arm— and the tattoo of a winding snake in black and red.

Then they were driving blind as a thick, blood-red fluid spread all over the windshield!

6 Target Practice

Frank frantically jammed on the brakes as he forced down the side window and leaned out to get a glimpse of what was ahead. Had the van cleared the gray hatchback? Was there other traffic in the street? He couldn't see through the gluey mess on the windshield.

The van skidded a little, coming to a stop just in front of a streetlight.

Joe had bailed out in midstop, jumping into the street after the gray car. As Frank stepped out he saw his brother in the middle of the block giving up his pursuit. The gray car had pulled a U-turn and roared off.

"Who *were* those guys?" Joe asked as he came up. "Nailing us like this just when we thought we'd shaken them off." He gestured in frustration at the windshield.

Frank had already gotten paper towels and window cleaner from the back of the van and began to clean the red gook from the windshield.

Joe came over to help. "What did they throw at us? A water balloon?"

"Something like that, but a little more sophisticated," Frank said. "This is definitely the most convincing 'stage blood' I've ever seen."

"Yeah—next time it will be real, right? And *ours.* I get the message. About as subtle as a steamroller." Joe stomped around, wiping the stuff up.

Frank was just as angry as he worked. He was furious over the attack on Mr. Watanabe, and now the attackers seemed to be taunting him. Still, this time, the attackers had left a clue. "Did you get a good look at the arm that threw this gunk at us? It had a tattoo on it."

"Right," said Joe, "a snake, an incredibly long one. It must have gone all the way from the guy's trigger finger to his elbow—maybe even farther. It was blood red and black."

The Hardys regarded each other.

"I guess we have proof that the Yakuza are definitely involved," Frank said. By this time he and Joe had finished cleaning the windshield and were ready to hit the road again. "Let's go find Jim Lao, and see if he can confirm what we already know."

Feeling more determined than ever, the boys drove back to the business district and found a parking space near the office of the *Bayport Times*.

They entered the orderly chaos of the city room, where dozens of desks were turned face-to-face, with reporters talking on phones, operating computer terminals, or clacking away on type-writers. Jim Lao had a desk in the midst of the madness, and he smiled when he saw the Hardys.

"You're lucky to find me here," Lao said. "I was supposed to be covering a corruption trial in a small island nation—but the government called it off. How's Fenton? And what can I do for Bayport's young sleuths?"

Frank explained that they were interested in finding out whatever they could about the Yakuza.

"For starters, do you recognize this?" asked Frank. He pulled from an envelope the scrap of silk from Mr. Watanabe's door frame.

"Kinshasu," said Lao, looking at the Hardys more sharply. "It's their symbol."

Spreading the scrap on his desk, Lao went on. "The Yakuza don't come in one big lump. They have different clans—some say up to twenty."

He shrugged. "I've met people from maybe a dozen or so clans in my time. Each has its own family business. But these guys"—Lao pushed the symbol back across the desk—"are up there with the top two or three Yakuza clans. The Kinshasu are very powerful."

"And what branch of crime is their 'family business,' as you call it?" asked Frank.

"Smuggling," came the terse reply. "The Kinshasu pride themselves on their ability to pay

54

off customs inspectors, to sneak across borders, to package deadly things innocently—they've got it down to a science. They're probably even computerized by now, with airline and freighter schedules shown right on the monitor."

"You're kidding!" said Joe.

"Nope. It's like a giant game of 'Button, button, who's got the button?'" He grinned. "Suppose the Kinshasu need to get a shipment of stolen buttons from Korea to this country. A friendly dock hand will stick them in with something else—a shipment of toys, maybe—and the Kinshasu will come up with a complicated shipping schedule."

He thought for a second. "It might go to Singapore, where a friendly customs agent will pass the buttons, and somebody else will ship them to Baltimore or Bayport. Our customs people may be on the lookout for buttons from Korea, and won't be looking for anything from Singapore —especially since the buttons are now officially part of a shipment of books, or something else."

"Incredible," Joe said.

"Have you heard of the Yakuza operating in this country?" Frank asked.

"There have been rumors in the last ten years or so. The Kinshasu probably have people in most of the major ports—New Orleans, New York, Chicago, Baltimore, Philadelphia, maybe even Bayport—it's on the Atlantic, and pretty close to New York Harbor. But all of it is rumor. Somebody pretty powerful must be looking out for them because there's been no hard evidence so far."

Lao called up a file on his computer. "These are my notes from a story that I haven't run yet. You can see"—he sped through a few pages on the screen, using the search function to highlight the word *Yakuza*—"there are lots of rumors. But no evidence. Nothing, so far, that I can print."

"You've given us a lot of background—and a lot of your time," Frank thanked the reporter.

"I don't suppose you'd like to tell me what this is all about?" asked Lao. "Or where you got that piece of silk?"

Frank shook his head. "You'll get the scoop when we have something concrete," he assured Lao. "But for now, the less said, the better."

"I understand." They shook hands, and the Hardys headed for their van—to find Paul Pierson leaning against the door.

Joe greeted Paul with a grin. "What's up?"

"I came downtown to the hospital—they wouldn't let me in," Paul said. "Then I spotted your van. I need to talk to someone."

The young karate champ held out an envelope to Frank, who pulled out a single sheet of paper.

"Hmmm," the older Hardy muttered. "Looks like our Yakuza buddies are up to their old tricks—anonymous-letter style this time." He held out the paper to Joe. It was messily assembled from words cut out of newspapers and magazines.

Joe read: " 'Checked in with your sensei lately? If you fight on Friday, you'll be his roommate.' "

"Nice," Joe remarked sarcastically, handing the note back to Frank. "When did it come?"

"Someone slipped it under the front door," Paul replied. "I don't understand it."

"Just don't let it shake you," said Frank encouragingly. "And thanks for bringing it by. We may be able to learn something from it—although I don't imagine the sender left prints."

"Or a return address," Joe said, smiling.

"I don't see what you can get from a page full of garbage," Paul complained.

"Even though it's all made up of cutout words and letters, it's still a possible lead," Joe said. "We once solved a whole case by tracking down the sources of cutout words."

"How did you do that?" asked Paul.

"Well, you know, printed typefaces are like footprints or even fingerprints—each one is different. And sometimes, to get a certain look for a magazine or book, a publisher will use an unusual typeface. We had a case with a ransom note in a certain typeface—and it turned out only one person involved was likely to have any magazines with that kind of print. He was an antiques dealer and got an antiques magazine with a specially designed headline type."

"How did you know *that?*" asked Paul. He was having a hard time deciding whether to be skeptical or amazed.

57

"There's an expert in Bayport," said Joe. "An old guy—retired printer, called Charles Harris. He's made a lifelong hobby of typefaces—he kind of collects them. We showed the letter to him, and he recognized the type right away. He dug around in his files and matched it."

"Wow!" said Paul. "Do you think that old Charlie Harris could find out something about this little love note?"

"He might—if any of this type is unusual enough," said Frank.

He and Paul put the letter on the side of the van, bending close to study it. Joe leaned back against the door on the driver's side and gazed up at the sky.

He blinked. Something was moving on the rooftop of the building across the parking lot. No, it was some*one*. Silhouetted in the bright sunlight, the person seemed to be dressed all in black. Joe grinned to himself. He was beginning to see ninjas everywhere.

Then the figure raised something to its shoulder. It was outlined against the sky for a moment, and Joe realized what he was seeing—a crossbow!

He pushed off from the door, yelling, *"Down!"* Frank and Paul turned in surprise as Joe dove for them.

But out of the corner of his eye, Joe caught the glint of a crossbow bolt, streaking toward them.

7 Department of Dirty Tricks

Joe rammed into Frank and Paul with barely an instant to spare. The bolt zipped right over him, close enough for him to feel the wind of its passing.

The stubby arrow thunked into the side of the van as the three boys tumbled to the sidewalk.

Frank and Joe rose quickly to their feet, Joe pointing up. "On the roof!" he cried.

The Hardys ran across the parking lot, Frank yelling over his shoulder to Paul, "Take cover behind the van!" They were all in the open, and if their attacker let loose another shot . . .

When they reached the side of the building, Joe leaped up to catch the bottom of the fire-escape ladder. Then they raced up, the rickety metal stairs rattling under their feet. Reaching the roof, they threw themselves into a dive and roll to confuse the enemy's aim. Jumping to their feet, they confronted . . . nothing.

"Nobody's here," Joe said in disbelief, scanning the wide-open space. The only possible hiding place was a shedlike structure whose door led into the building and down the stairs.

Frank and Joe split up to circle the shack but found no one on the other side. Joe rattled the rusty old chain and padlock on the door. "Nobody escaped this way," he said.

"And he didn't go down the fire-escape steps as we were coming up," Frank said. "So where is he?"

"He must have scaled down the other side," said Joe.

"Let's see if he left any traces." Frank started across the roof. He found no sign of the crossbow but got one reward for his efforts. On one sun-softened section of the tarred roof, someone had left footprints. The pattern looked like a sneaker tread, with dots and circles clearly marked.

"What was the guy wearing?" Frank asked as the Hardys headed back down the fire escape to the parking lot.

"I can't be sure—he was against the sun," Joe said. "But I think he was in black."

"Another ninja? Wearing sneakers?" Frank frowned.

"And starting to play a little dirtier," Joe added.

They came back to the van, where Paul was studying the stubby arrow. "Talk about close calls," he said. "What kind of bow does that guy have? He was pretty far away."

Joe chuckled grimly. "A crossbow—more powerful than the archery sets we played with back in summer camp."

Frank took a look at the bolt.

"Standard hunting equipment," he said. "You could buy this at any sporting-goods store. I'd like a look at that bow, though. I bet it wasn't standard!"

"Look, guys, I've got to go," Paul said. "Not that it hasn't been exciting enough." He started down the street.

"Hey, Paul," Joe said. "What about the match?"

"You don't think I'm going to let a little thing like this stand in my way, do you?" Paul called back. "See you guys." He took off.

Frank looked thoughtful. "Remember what you said on the way down, Joe? About people playing dirty? Who do we know who's famous for doing that?"

Joe nodded. "Who also has a really big collection of strange weapons." He jumped into the van.

Frank got into the driver's seat, still frowning. "I can't see Keith going as far as nearly murdering someone to get him out of his way," he said.

"Even so, I think it's time we asked him some questions." Joe got out the mobile phone. "Start the van, Frank. I've got to find out where Keith lives."

It took a couple of minutes' calling around to get Keith's address, but soon they were on their

61

way. As Frank drove, Joe acted as navigator, leading his brother through the streets of Burnham.

"I'm beginning to wonder about this trip," Frank said as they turned off Farning Avenue. "Why would Keith Owen shoot at us?"

"I'm not sure he was shooting at us at all," Joe told him.

"You mean he was aiming for Paul, to make sure he doesn't compete on Friday?" Frank shook his head.

"No, just *near* Paul." Joe propped his feet up on the dash and squinted into the bright sunlight. "I keep running the scene through my head. I tackled you guys, the crossbow bolt went over my head. I think it was aimed right between you two, at the paper you'd spread out."

"So now we're dealing with a paper-killer," Frank said sarcastically. "Or another warning— and you think it's aimed at Paul."

"Maybe Keith is trying to take advantage of the situation to scare Paul off," Joe suggested.

"We'll just have to find out," Frank said as he pulled up in front of a typical suburban house— white with green trim. The matching garage was anything but typical. Since the door was open, the Hardys could see that Keith had turned it into a workout room. Barbells and weights were scattered around the floor, and in one corner was a universal gym. Against the back wall was a pegboard, hung with all sorts of unusual weapons: old-fashioned swords, a machete, dueling pistols, even a blowgun with darts from South America. There was no crossbow in the collection.

"Hey, it's the Hardly boys," Keith said sneeringly as Frank and Joe entered the garage. "I read all about you in the papers. What hot case are you on now? Somebody lose a cat or something?" He didn't pause in his sit-ups as he spoke.

"No, it's something you might be able to help us with," Frank said, trying to hold on to his temper.

Keith didn't answer, turning his back to the boys and going for a barbell.

"What have you been up to all day, Keith?" asked Joe. His eyes were fixed on an empty hook on the pegboard—where a bow might have hung.

"This." Keith's answer came in a burst of exhaled breath as he hoisted the weight. "I've been practicing karate all day. Don't want to waste all night pulverizing that punk Pierson on Friday."

"How do you know you'll make the finals?" asked Frank.

Keith dropped the barbell. "You trying to psych me out, or something. I *know* who'll win."

"Sounds to me like you're whistling in the dark," Joe said.

"Pierson might be okay," Keith said, "but he's nothing to worry about. Look at his trainer. The guy's supposed to be a big karate hotshot from Japan, but he couldn't even protect himself when somebody broke into his dojo. You think I should be afraid of this loser's student?"

Frank could hear the blood pounding in his ears. What right had this creep, who used his skills to bully people, to say anything about the sensei? Mr. Watanabe had more of the spirit of karate in his little finger than Keith would ever have.

"Oh, that's right, you're one of Mr. What-a-nerdy's students, too." Keith laughed nastily.

Joe watched as Frank took a step forward, his face white with rage.

"Did I hurt your feelings?" Keith taunted. "Maybe you want to go a round with the swords. No, maybe something more your speed—like hopscotch."

"I was thinking of something more like an archery contest," Frank snapped back.

Keith suddenly turned his back on them. "Well, go play Robin Hood somewhere else."

"Come on," said Joe. The boys turned on their heels and headed for the van.

On the drive back home, Frank soon calmed down. He and Joe both knew better than to let crude insults like Keith's cloud their thinking. Joe turned up the radio loud, and the boys sang along at the tops of their lungs. A good way to let off steam, thought Joe.

The loud music on the radio nearly drowned

64

out the beep of their mobile phone. Frank quickly switched off the music while Joe grabbed the receiver.

"Joe, it's Tikko," said the caller. "I'm at Uncle Seino's house. I've finished translating the notes and letter—can you meet me here?"

"Right away." As soon as he hung up Joe started giving new navigation to Frank.

They reached the sensei's house in eight minutes flat. Tikko was in the living room waiting for them.

"For starters," she said, producing the calendar, "I didn't see anything interesting in this—even though it took me a while to figure it out. At first I thought it was nonsense. The words don't exist in Japanese. It was only when I started sounding out the Japanese characters that things started to make sense." She held up a list of Japanese words. "Here's the symbol for king, followed by the sign for grave. This one means castle, and this one means hill. . . ."

"Castle Hill!" Frank leaned forward. "King—grave . . . Kingsbury! What else is on the list?"

"Redcliff, Riverton . . . Here's the whole list, in English." Tikko handed over another sheet of paper. "They're just towns up and down the East Coast."

"Why would he have translated them?" asked Joe.

"Who knows?" said Tikko. "Maybe he had to

write to friends back home in Japan who were coming here for a visit or something. It's not important. But *this* is." Tikko held out the document that the boys had found taped under the sensei's desk, along with a translation. Her face was calm, but the papers shook in her hand.

Joe took the translation from her and scanned it quickly.

"The letter must be a fake," Joe said, even while he was still reading.

"No. The paper you gave me was definitely in my uncle's handwriting. See how we were all fooled!" She fought back tears.

Silently, Joe handed the translation to Frank. His brother had always looked up to Mr. Watanabe. How would he react to this?

Frank read:

Esteemed Colleagues:

I the undersigned, Seino Watanabe, Sensei, do hereby pledge my solemn allegiance to the most exalted clan of **SHIKURA**, third degree of **YAKUZA**.

I do solemnly promise to fulfill those obligations contracted to me by the **SHIKURA**.

To this purpose I sign, pledging with the honor accruing to my family name and the honor of a sensei.

Seino Watanabe

Frank stared down at his hands as they crumpled the translation. It couldn't be true! How could the sensei have joined a gang of ruthless criminals?

His hands tightened on the wad of paper. Could Mr. Watanabe himself be a killer?

8 No More Mr. Nice Guy

Frank tossed the crumpled paper on the desk. "There must be some explanation," he said.

"Sure." Tikko's voice was as tight as her face. "My uncle—so rich and powerful, living in a fancy house in a fancy part of Tokyo—got those things as rewards for being a killer. A—"

"Wait a minute, Tikko, let's think this through," Joe cut her off. "We can't deny that he was involved with the Yakuza somehow. But that doesn't necessarily mean he was a killer."

"You've got a point," said Frank, with a hint of gratitude in his voice.

The three started trying to make some sense of the letter, instead of being upset about it.

"Okay. He was a sensei back then—and a national hero," said Frank. "And he was probably using his karate skills for the Yakuza."

"As a hired killer," Tikko said flatly.

"Maybe not," Frank urged. "There are other

jobs. Maybe he was a bodyguard. Or maybe he was just a sensei for them, too. He might have only trained their people."

"That's not much better." Tikko's face was stubborn.

"He may not have had any choice," Joe said. "They probably forced him somehow."

Tikko pointed to the letter. "My uncle swore *on his honor.* He would never do that unless he meant it. This isn't scout's honor," she said. " 'Honor' means something much more serious in Japan. If you lose your honor the only way out is death."

"Suppose he didn't know who they were," Frank suggested. "I'll bet when he found out, he tried to quit—to walk away from the deal. That made them mad. They burned his house— maybe did other things. So he fled Japan and came here."

"He would have made sure about them before he promised," Tikko said doubtfully. "But it is a possibility."

"Maybe they finally tracked him down," Joe said. "No, that doesn't work. It doesn't really look as though he were hiding. Maybe they want him back," he suggested. "They probably knew where he was—Jim Lao said the Yakuza had been rumored to be active in this country for at least ten years."

Tikko's scowl returned. "Uncle Seino has lived here for ten years. Coincidence?"

"Probably," said Frank. "Relax, Tikko."

She crossed the room and sat down, defiantly putting her feet on the coffee table. Frank took a seat at the sensei's desk. He idly flipped through the folder of clippings about the karate meets. This was the Mr. Watanabe he knew—carefully keeping in touch with the whole karate world.

Suddenly a word caught his eye.

"Tikko, let me see that translation from Mr. Watanabe's calendar," Frank asked.

Tikko looked surprised but handed over the list of town names.

Frank read them over, sifting through the clippings. "Kingsbury, Castle Hill, Redcliff—they match," he said. "The towns on the calendar are the same as the towns where Oteman is running karate matches."

"He *is* a karate instructor," said Tikko bitterly. "I hardly think that's a clue."

"But why did he write them in Japanese?" asked Frank. "These names don't even exist in Japanese, right? He had to make up a translation for them—almost like a code name to himself. Most people who read Japanese wouldn't recognize the names, because they're not real Japanese words. And nobody who reads English would get it either."

Tikko looked at Frank with respect. "I didn't even think of that, of course—but you're right! When I read them, they made no sense."

"Why should he bother to make up a translation?" asked Joe. "Unless it was a code? He must

70

have thought there was something going on at the karate matches that he didn't like."

"I know how we can find out," said Tikko. "The president of Oteman—the company that sponsors the matches—knows my uncle. His name is Mr. Tanaka. Why don't we ask him?"

"Good idea," said Frank. He grabbed a phone directory and quickly looked up the number for the offices of Oteman, Inc. "Give him a call, Tikko." He read out the phone number from the book.

Tikko dialed, listened for a moment, then said, "Mr. Tanaka's office, please." She put her hand over the mouthpiece. "It's ringing."

Then she said, "Tikko Shinsura for Mr. Tanaka —he knows my uncle, Seino Watanabe." Tikko frowned. "Oh, I see. You don't know when he'll be back? No, I can't leave a phone number." She hung up. "He's out of the office."

"So I guessed," Frank said.

Joe thumped his hand on the desk. "Let's pay him a visit," he suggested.

"Okay," Frank said. "We can tell him about what happened to the sensei."

As they headed for the van Joe said, "You know, Frank, we'll go right by Charlie Harris's place on the way to Oteman. Let's drop off Paul's little love note and see what he can tell us about those glued-on letters."

"Good thinking," said Frank. Tikko looked mystified, so Joe quickly explained about Paul's anonymous letter and about their helpful hobby-ist, Charles Harris.

The route to Oteman took them past the old man's "office"—a converted barn behind his house.

They stepped inside to find Charlie's "files"—piles upon piles of newspapers and magazines.

"I don't know how he does it," Frank said, "but Charlie knows exactly where everything is. He won't even let them be dusted, in case someone messes up the order."

But if the papers were dusty, the printing press in the middle of the room was spotless and shining. A short, round man stepped from behind the machine, smiling. "Frank! Joe! Got another mystery for me?"

The smile disappeared as he read the note and heard the story. "Looks like local stuff—maybe cut out from that string of countywide papers. I'll have to look more carefully and get back to you."

"Thanks, Charlie," said Frank. "Phone us in the van if it's important." Charlie waved goodbye as they climbed back into the van. Soon the three were speeding out to Oteman.

"That's one lead checked out. Maybe we'll get something from Mr. Tanaka. We also have karate business to talk about with him," Frank said. "There's the question about Paul's eligibility." He filled Tikko in briefly on the rules of sponsorship. "So, if Paul doesn't have a sensei there, he may not be allowed to compete."

72

"Maybe I can be his sponsor," said Tikko brightly. "I am family, you know."

"Thanks, Tikko, but I don't know if that will work." Then Frank smiled. "But it's a good excuse to start talking with Mr. Tanaka."

They had almost reached the headquarters of Oteman in the hilly country just outside Bayport. Somehow, the conversation had come around to Mr. Watanabe and the Yakuza.

"None of the connections we've come up with sounds too good," Joe said. "If only Mr. Watanabe were awake and able to tell us . . ."

He cut off his words as he looked out the back windows. "Uh-oh," Joe said. "Don't look now, but our pals in the little gray hatchback are behind us." He inched toward the rear of the van for a better view.

Frank glanced in the rearview mirror. Sure enough, just fifty yards back was the same sedan that had tailed them in Bayport.

Frank pressed harder on the gas. "Hang on, Tikko," he said. "We don't want to play tag with these guys on this road. Seat belt on?"

"Of course. Quit worrying about me."

"Okay," said Frank, flooring the gas pedal.

The van shot forward, its engine roaring.

A noise also came from the dashboard—a loud *FFFFFFTTT!*

"What was that?" asked Joe. He turned to look at Frank—and saw his brother writhing in his seat, both hands over his eyes.

Tikko cried out, "The wheel!"

"My eyes are burning!" Frank yelled.

Joe's gaze was glued to the van's steering wheel, with no one guiding it. He scrambled to get back near the front seats.

The van reached the top of the hill and started down a steep, winding road. Even as Tikko grabbed the wheel, they began to careen faster and faster. She tried to stretch a foot over to the brakes as they sped around a curve.

An unbelievable sight met them: a huge tanker truck blocked the road—a truck filled with gasoline.

If they didn't stop the car, they would be heading straight for a fiery death!

9 Business as Usual?

Joe reached around his brother, grabbing the wheel from Tikko. "Hit the brakes!" he cried. Tikko managed to get her foot over to the brake pedal, which was still covered by Frank's foot. Jamming down on Frank's toes, she managed to slow the van as Joe twisted the wheel.

They skidded off the road, just missing the stalled truck. After bouncing along the shoulder for a few yards, the van came to a halt with its nose in some bushes, only a few feet from a steep ravine.

Still rubbing his eyes and coughing, Frank jumped out of the van and took several deep breaths. Tikko climbed out after him. The driver of the gasoline truck rushed over as Joe handed Frank a canteen of water, helping him wash out his eyes.

"You kids all right?" the driver asked. "We all nearly got killed. Some crazy guys whipped past me on this curve and shot out my tires. I was afraid to move—and then you people came along."

"This wasn't the best place in the world to stop," said Joe.

"Had to check I wasn't riding too low—one spark with this load . . ."

"I know," Joe told the driver. "We almost found out."

"Right," the driver agreed. "You sure you're okay? Your pal looks pretty upset."

Heavy tears were still rolling down from Frank's eyes. "We're fine, really."

"I'd better move my truck before we have another accident," the driver said. "You need help with your van?"

Joe shook his head. "Thanks, we can handle it."

As the truck rumbled off, Frank leaned into the van, searching under the dashboard. "Look at this," he said, detaching something. It was a little capsule, like a CO_2 cartridge but smaller. "Taped under the dash. And look at the nozzle—a little radio-controlled spray."

Frank's face was grim. "Very cute. They have two cars tailing us so we wouldn't tumble. One car goes ahead and sets up the accident. The other one comes up behind us, presses a button, this stuff squirts out, and we're driving blind."

"What is it?" Tikko asked.

"Your guess is as good as mine," Frank replied. "I'm just glad it's not permanent."

"Any sign of our friends?" asked Joe, looking around the curve.

"They'll be long gone," Frank called after him. "No point in hanging around for an 'accident.'"

"These guys sure play hardball," said Tikko. "But I guess the famous detectives of Bayport are up to the challenge." She grinned at them.

"So far, at least," Frank said. "Let's go."

The three climbed back into the van, and in just a few minutes they were nearing their original destination. From the top of a hill half a mile from the company headquarters, they could make out the lettering on the warehouse: Oteman, Inc. Import/Export. Next to the sign was painted the company logo—a huge red and black dragon.

As they drove down the hill they saw that the warehouse was only part of a much larger complex covering a good three acres. There were more storage areas, with busy loading docks serving dozens of trucks. Workmen scurried from building to building. Joe noticed a lot of the people out in the open wore gray uniforms and spoke into walkie-talkies—guards.

One of the gray-clad men met them at the visitors' gate and directed them to a small office building in the middle of the complex. Frank parked the van in front and went in with Joe and Tikko.

After taking their names, the receptionist made a quick phone call.

"Mr. Tanaka," she said, "there is a Tikko

Shinsura here to see you, with two young gentlemen." The woman looked up in surprise at Tikko
as she hung up the phone. "He says he'll be
pleased to see you in the main warehouse. This
way."

She stood up and led them to a door that
connected the office quarters with the large
warehouse.

The warehouse was a vast, busy space. Despite
the huge number of boxes and crates everywhere,
the place felt cavernous and empty. Forklift
trucks moved boxes from one pile to another, and
everywhere were uniformed men with hard hats
and clipboards. They appeared to be taking a
count.

A dapper middle-aged man broke away from a
group and strode over to the Hardys and Tikko.
Mr. Tanaka, who was of medium height, wore a
perfectly tailored conservative blue suit. Everything about him—from the horn-rimmed glasses
on his square face to the carefully styled glossy
black hair—bespoke a high-powered business-
man.

The smile he gave Tikko was warm as he
stretched out his hand to greet her.

"Miss Shinsura," he said, bowing. "I was dev-
astated to hear the news of your uncle. How is
he?"

"Not well, I'm afraid," said Tikko. "They've
moved him out of the intensive-care ward, but
he's still unconscious. The doctors are hoping

that won't last too long." Tikko turned to the Hardys. "These are my friends, Joe and Frank Hardy."

"I'm also one of Mr. Watanabe's students," Frank began. "Since your company is in charge of the tournament at the end of the week, I thought we should come and talk to you."

Frank wanted to learn more about the whole tournament situation, and he figured this was the best way to lead into it. "I know the regulations say a student must be sponsored by a sensei," he went on. "But since Mr. Watanabe can't be there, will you agree to let Tikko be our entry's sponsor? His name is Paul Pierson."

Mr. Tanaka's smile stayed in place, but his eyes became thoughtful. "Ordinarily, we require a recognized sensei to be a student's sponsor," he said. "But under the circumstances, I think we can waive it. Tikko, I would be happy to have you act as Paul's sponsor. I've heard of him. He's a very talented boy and deserves to be there. I will alert the competitors from the other towns so that there is no problem."

"That's great, Mr. Tanaka," Frank said gratefully. "We appreciate your help. This whole tournament is really exciting—especially the idea of the demonstration tour in Japan. I was sort of curious—why did you and your company get involved?"

Mr. Tanaka looked at Frank for a moment, straight-faced, then smiled again. "My young friend—isn't it obvious?" Tanaka gestured at the huge warehouse around him. "My company is in the business of importing and exporting goods. There are many things to buy with a dollar—or a yen. But there are two things that cannot be bought—understanding and good will."

He spread his arms. "The karate tour—like many other activities that my company has sponsored in the past—will promote those things. I call them *intangibles*. They cannot be seen or touched, counted, or computed as profit. But they are crucial to my way of doing business."

Tanaka finished his speech with a little smile of satisfaction.

Tikko looked impressed, but Frank was a bit skeptical. Finally, Joe asked, "Isn't this trip a little expensive? I mean all the regional champions will be going, and that means buying a dozen round-trip tickets."

"An investment, Joe." Tanaka's smile started looking forced, especially when he noticed one of his workers trying to get his attention. He took Tikko by the elbow and began to lead the three teenagers toward the door. Frank was reminded of a polite host whose dinner guests had stayed too long. The Hardys and Tikko found themselves being ushered gracefully but firmly out.

"I wish I had more time to chat," Tanaka apologized. "But the work . . ."

"Well, thanks very much for your time," said Frank, taking one last look around. "And by the way—how did the other matches go? Well? Any surprises?"

Mr. Tanaka lifted an eyebrow. "Nothing special," he said. "Although we did see a lot of talent."

"I wonder how Paul would match up with your other winners?" Joe asked.

"I'll have a chance to see Friday at the match," said Mr. Tanaka. "You kids run along. My cordial regards to your father, Miss Shinsura." He bowed briefly, then turned to talk to a man with a clipboard.

"Well, we've been definitely dismissed," Frank said as they walked toward the van. They reached it and climbed in. "Tikko, pass me that folder, would you?" he asked from the backseat. She gave him the manila folder from the glove compartment.

"What are you up to, Frank?" asked Joe.

"I'm trying to figure out why Mr. Tanaka was so helpful—but managed to tell us nothing," Frank answered.

"He sure didn't seem to want to talk about the other matches," agreed Tikko.

Frank reached for the phone and began to dial.

"Who are you calling?" asked Tikko.

"The newspaper in Redcliff," Frank replied, tapping in the phone number. "That's where the last match was held."

He got the main switchboard. "Local sports, please." A pause, then he started talking. "My name is Frank Hardy—I'm doing a story for the *Bayport High Sentinel*. That's right, a school paper. Well, it's about the problems of champions —why does the stress of winning and losing make some would-be champs choke. I'm checking with some local papers and heard you had karate regionals in your town. I'd like to know the usual stuff: Who won? Was the winner the odds-on favorite? What was the match like?"

Joe and Tikko listened quietly. After posing his first round of questions, Frank grabbed a pen, scribbling notes on the folder. "Interesting," he said a few times. Then, "Thanks. I'll be in touch tomorrow."

He hung up the phone. "The match was a forfeit," he told Joe and Tikko. "The person who was favored to win had to drop out at the last minute—he was hurt in a car accident."

Joe caught his breath. From the look in Frank's eye, they were both thinking the same thing. "An accident?" asked the younger Hardy.

"Maybe. Maybe not," said Frank. "I think it would be a good idea to check out the other matches as well."

He dialed the newspaper in Kingsbury, then the one in Castle Hill. All the conversations went much the same way. A girl had been expected to win in Kingsbury, but she fell down a ravine on the morning of the match. Instead of competing, she was in a hospital, getting stitches. The favorite in Castle Hill had suffered an accident, too.

Frank passed on the information, frowning.

"Three accidents?" said Joe. "I smell a rat."

"A whole pack of them," Frank said. "What worries me is that they may go beyond accidents to stop Paul Pierson."

He stared at Joe. "They may try to kill him!"

10 On the Road Again

Joe Hardy was grim as he drove the van through the early-morning traffic the next day. The danger to Paul seemed to grow with every piece of information they found.

Worse, Paul wouldn't listen to any warnings. Joe and Frank had put in a long night, figuring what to do next. They'd finally decided to visit the unsuccessful front-runners in the nearest towns. Had they received threats like Paul?

Tikko had called, insisting on coming along when she heard their plan. As they drove up to her house she was already standing by the road. An hour's drive brought them to Redcliff, where they quickly found the local newspaper. Another crowded city room greeted their eyes. Alec Wescott, a short, red-faced reporter, handled the local sports beat.

"I thought it seemed pretty strange at the time," he remarked. "Scott Bauman was favored to win by a long shot. There was no way Ray Newton was going to beat him. Then suddenly, Scott's out and Ray's got the title—and the trip to Japan."

"So what's this guy Ray like?" asked Joe.

"I don't actually know him very well," said Alec, "but he's not winning any personality awards. Scott was really looking forward to the trip—he'd been studying Japanese for about four years, now he had a chance to use it. So when he was dropped from the match, it was a big disappointment. Ray really rubbed his nose in it. Told him to go back to driver's-ed. class."

"Nice guy," said Frank.

"Sounds like he could be Keith's long lost brother," said Joe.

"Where can we find Scott Bauman?" asked Frank.

"He's usually at the dojo this time of day," said Alec. "Right down at the end of this street, take a left. You can't miss it. It's just a few yards down from the big red-brick armory building."

"Thanks a lot." Frank, Joe, and Tikko headed outside, down Redcliff's main street. All the buildings were brick with green tile roofs—even the dojo looked like an old-fashioned British store.

They entered to find a lanky blond guy leading the beginner students in exercises—Scott Bauman.

"His moves are good, but his heart isn't in it," Tikko whispered. Frank nodded.

85

Scott glanced toward them curiously as he continued the class. When the exercises ended, he came over to them. "Can I help you?"

"We were hoping you could tell us a little about the regional karate championships," Frank said.

"Well, it's no secret that the favorites haven't been winning their matches," said Scott. "I don't have any hard feelings toward Ray, but I think I got a stinking break."

"That's what we think, too." Frank briefly filled Scott in on the events in Bayport. "We'd like to know more about your car accident."

Scott's eyes flickered. "I'm sorry to hear about this attack on your uncle," he said to Tikko. "But I'm sure it has nothing to do with me."

"Lots of other people lost their chance at the championships through accidents—too many," Joe told him. "Do you think what happened to you was just dumb luck?"

"That's *exactly* what I think," snapped Scott. "Incredibly dumb, stupid luck. I was driving in the rain, my car hit an oily patch, and I crashed. That's all. Now, if you'll excuse me, I have a class to lead." He turned his back on the Hardys, resuming the class.

The conversation over, the Hardys and Tikko took their leave. They had Scott's side of the story, at least. An oily patch in the road? That could be sabotage. Then why was Scott keeping quiet about it?

"He seemed to get rattled easily," remarked Tikko as they headed down the street.

"Yeah—like your uncle was rattled," recalled Frank. "Let's see what we can dig up in Kingsbury."

Kingsbury was just an hour's drive farther up from Redcliff. The three teenagers spent the time going over what they knew.

"Suppose Scott had been threatened like my uncle—and your friend Paul," Tikko suggested. "That would explain why he wouldn't talk to us."

"And I don't think what we told him helped any," Frank said. "We've had more luck getting the details from the newspaper people."

"Let's see what luck we have at the *Kingsbury Courier*," Joe said. "We have a twelve o'clock appointment with their sports guy."

Just outside the town, however, traffic came to a near standstill.

"What's holding us up?" Tikko asked.

"The U.S. Army," Joe answered. "I suppose it's the National Guard. They've got a convoy of troop trucks turning onto this road." He sighed. "Making the most unbelievable traffic jam."

"Let's go another way," said Frank.

"The paper office is on this road," Joe pointed out. "Look at the map."

Tikko peered through the windshield. "Have we declared war or something?" she asked, pointing to the solemn-looking soldiers on the troop truck.

"Well, I guess National Guard duty isn't like going out on a picnic," Joe said.

"At least *we* have some civilian comforts," said

Frank, popping a cassette into the player. They rode out the rest of the traffic jam to music.

It was three minutes after twelve when they finally reached the newspaper's offices. When they found the reporter who covered local sports, she had pretty much the same story as Alec Wescott had given them in Redcliff. A strong favorite had been put out of commission, and the title had gone to someone else.

The favorite was a girl named Holly Stevenson, and the reporter even phoned her to introduce the Hardys. Holly hesitated to talk for a moment, then asked them to meet her at the mall, where she would show them the scene of the fall that had taken her out of competition.

The meeting place was a pizza joint—Frank, Joe, and Tikko were hungrily digging into a pie when a young girl came in to grab a soda. It was easy to see that Holly was an athlete—tall and strongly built, she moved gracefully and energetically, despite a very stiff left knee.

"Holly?" Frank asked, standing up.

"Hi—you're the guys I'm supposed to meet?"

Frank, Joe, and Tikko introduced themselves, then got right to the point.

"My accident happened right here—I work nights at the jeans shop," Holly explained. "I was headed home after work. My car was in the lower level of the garage, and I didn't want to wait for the elevator. It takes forever. So I took the stairs, as I usually do."

She shrugged. "One minute I'm walking down the stairs. The next, I'm flying."

"You fell?" Tikko asked.

"Someone helped me." Holly rolled up one leg of her jeans to show them a very faint bruise line at her ankle. "Almost gone now, but you can still see it."

"A trip wire," Joe said. "Where did this happen?"

Holly took them away from the bright colors of the pizza parlor and down a gloomy staircase to show them the spot. "It was even darker than this," she explained. "One of the overhead bulbs had been smashed. But it wasn't the dark that made me trip."

"No, this would be a perfect place to set up a wire," Frank agreed.

"Did you find it?" asked Joe.

"No—when I came to, the security people made me go to the hospital for stitches. And by the next morning, when I finally had a chance to get back here, there was no trace of the wire."

Frank and Joe spread out over the garage, looking for anything out of the ordinary. As Joe checked out the level where Holly had been heading, he stopped short. "Hey, guys," he called. "Take a look."

Frank stared. "Footprints? In a garage?"

Several of the yellow lines between the parking spaces were smudged. Smeared on the floor, faint but still readable, was a sneaker tread—a pattern of dots and circles.

"Just like on the roof where the guy tried to use us for target practice," Joe said.

"When were these lines painted?" Frank asked.

Holly stared. "On the day of my fall. I remember because the smell of the paint nearly made me pass out again."

"Maybe the people who set you up weren't so smart to make this place so dark," Tikko said.

"Didn't the cops notice this?" Frank asked Holly.

The girl only shrugged.

"They started treating the whole thing as a mugging—till they found that whoever did it didn't touch my wallet. I had just been paid."

"Let me guess," Joe said. "After that, they just treated it as some kind of accident."

"Sounds familiar," Frank said. He looked at her seriously. "Before the match, did you get any threatening letters?"

Holly stared and thought for a moment before answering. "I almost forgot! It was weeks before the accident. At the time, I thought the letter was just some kind of joke. I just threw it out. It was like something out of an old movie—cutout newspaper letters pasted together."

"Sounds *very* familiar," said Joe. "Thanks for helping us, Holly. Maybe you'd like to come down to Riverton to see how Paul does."

"*If* he gets to compete," said Holly. "No, forget I said that. I'd love to come. Thanks."

She saw them back to their van and waved

goodbye as they headed off. They hadn't even gotten out of Kingsbury before Frank picked up the phone, dialing Paul Pierson.

"Paul? Frank. No, listen. We've just been talking to some of the other people who got cheated out of their places in the championships. One even got a threatening letter like yours. There's something really rotten about this whole thing. Be careful, Paul—be really on your guard."

"And if you see any guys in black outfits with samurai swords, *run!*" Joe called over from behind the steering wheel.

"Joke if you like," Frank said, hanging up the phone. "But I'll feel better when we're back in Bayport—close enough to help Paul if he needs us."

The rest of the ride home was a swirling conversation about Yakuza, ninjas, and threats. "It's like we were dealing with two sets of people," Joe said at one point. "There are the guys in that gray hatchback—very dangerous, very deadly. Then there's the gang that can't shoot straight, leaving footprints and clues."

"I just don't see why big-time criminals would get involved in the karate championships," Tikko said. "In other sports they might be betting, but not here. Maybe they were after my uncle—but why threaten your friend Paul? And why would they involve themselves all up and down the East Coast?"

"We've got lots of questions, and no answers," Frank said as they reached the outskirts of

91

Bayport. "Maybe we should stop by the hospital and check on the sensei. If he's awake, he might be able to clear up a lot of problems."

"Great idea," said Tikko.

"I'll drop you guys off and put the van in the lot," Joe volunteered, turning the van toward the hospital. "He can only have two visitors at a time, anyway."

Joe pulled up at the hospital entrance, and Tikko and Frank climbed out. Then Joe drove around the building and turned into the parking lot. As he pulled around the corner he caught the full effect of a gorgeous orange sunset—right in the eyes.

Joe carefully picked a spot that faced away from the sun. He looked at the hospital building, painted with orange light and shadows. Then one of the shadows moved.

"I don't believe it!" Joe said to himself. He stared into the patch of shadow again. Looking carefully, he could make out a figure, dressed all in black, sliding down a rope hanging from the hospital roof. It was a ninja! And he could only have one destination—Mr. Watanabe's room!

Joe quickly realized he'd never reach the front door of the hospital in time to stop the ninja. He'd have to do the best he could. Leaning on the horn, Joe began sounding out a warning in Morse code: S-O-S N-I-N-J-A S-O-S. He repeated the message twice, hoping it would carry to within the hospital. Even as he honked he watched helplessly as the figure opened a window and slid through.

"Uncle Seino is in room five-twenty," Tikko told Frank as they stepped out of the hospital elevator. "Let's stop at the nurses' station first and find out how he is."

The nurse on duty looked up with a scowl on her face. "Who's making that racket with his horn!" she said. "Doesn't he know enough to keep quiet in a hospital zone?"

The loud honking suddenly got quieter, as if a window had been closed. But Frank had already caught the long-short-long message. S-O-S— help! "I think that's Joe," he told Tikko. "You check with the nurse. I'll check on the sensei!"

He rushed down the hall, counting off room numbers.

Throwing open the door of Room 520, he found a black-clad figure with a hypodermic needle in his hand, leaning over Mr. Watanabe. Frank saw the needle was full—the assassin hadn't had time to do his dirty work.

A loud voice behind Frank started to say, "What's going—"

The ninja dropped the needle and ran for the door. He rammed Frank into the outraged nurse, then started running down the hallway.

The yells and screams of other hospital staff members told Frank which way his quarry had headed. He reached the fire stairs before the door had even swung closed behind the ninja.

As Frank raced up the stairway he could hear feet pounding ahead of him. Pouring on a burst of speed, he even caught a glimpse of the black-clad figure whipping around the next flight of stairs.

Frank reached the roof, to find the ninja searching frantically for an avenue of escape— but the building was an isolated one, and they were six stories up.

The ninja whirled at Frank's first charge, whipping out a kick. It was a clumsy attack. Frank blocked and landed a chop to the guy's shoulder. The ninja retreated, and Frank landed a kick as well, knocking the assassin right back to the low parapet on the roof.

The ninja jumped up on the low wall. Then, as Frank charged to grab him, he dodged out of the way, giving Frank a push toward the edge.

Frank's arms swung wildly as his knees banged into the parapet. The whole world seemed frozen in time. His hands reached down desperately for a handhold, but his momentum had carried him too far forward.

Then Frank was falling—plunging headfirst off the roof!

11 Too Close for Comfort

Instinctively, Frank's hands swept out as he fell through the air, feeling for anything to hold. His hand brushed something—a rope! The ninja's climbing rope—it was still in place! Frank grabbed, holding on for dear life as the thin rope cut into his hand. Below him the ground seemed to spin sickeningly.

Gently Frank moved his feet along the side of the building, feeling for a toehold. Finally, he found a gap between two bricks. Frank put half his weight on it and began to inch his way up the rope, which was secured to the roof parapet by a three-pronged metal claw. He had only a foot to go, but at this range the metal claw was likely to shift any moment, so Frank moved with great care.

At least the ninja hadn't looked over to see him. Otherwise the guy would probably be sawing at the rope.

Finally, Frank could see over the parapet. His right arm reached out and grabbed the inner edge, and he hoisted himself to safety. Just as he found himself on solid ground, the roof door opened, and Tikko rushed out, followed by a panting Joe.

"What's your hurry?" asked Frank breathlessly as he dusted himself off.

"I had to run all the way from the parking lot," Joe told him.

"Are you okay?" Tikko asked.

"Sure, except for a few scrapes and scratches. I look more like I was fighting with somebody's pet cat instead of a ninja. Speaking of which, where did our friend go?"

Joe was already searching the roof. "Disappeared," he said. "I think he must have gone down the fire escape."

The three of them headed downstairs again. "At least nothing happened to my uncle," Tikko reported. "The ninja didn't have a chance to use that hypodermic."

"And I want to make sure he doesn't get any more chances," Frank said. "It's time for a word in Con Riley's ear. With what we know now, I think he'll put a guard back—and maybe keep an eye on Paul as well."

"What's our next move?" Joe asked.

"I hoped you guys would stay around for a while," Tikko said, looking at her watch. "My father is due here to visit Uncle Seino."

"Great!" said Joe. "This might be a chance

to talk to him about that box Mr. Watanabe sent."

"I looked for it last night," Tikko told them. "It's in none of Dad's usual hiding places—I don't even think it's in the house."

As they sat in the waiting room Frank frowned in thought. "You know, Joe, that whole scene on the roof reminded me of something you said."

"Look before you leap?" Joe said with a grin.

"No—about the two teams of bad guys involved in the case. There was something not quite right about that ninja," said Frank. "I should have been *gone*. Ninjas are highly trained killers. They live and breathe karate. It's all they ever do. But I almost had that guy. Paul *definitely* would have had him."

"You mean you think he's not a good ninja?" Tikko asked. "Maybe he's still learning."

"So they sent in the B Team," Joe joked.

"That's just it," said Frank. "These guys swing back and forth. Some of the ninjas were good enough to take out Mr. Watanabe. Some haven't acted like ninjas at all."

"Okay," said Joe. "Then why the costumes?"

"Who knows?" said Frank. "Maybe they dress up to scare everyone. They sure know a *few* moves. But they're just not that good."

"Uh-oh, sounds like tough criticism," said a booming voice.

"Hi, Dad," said Tikko, jumping up. Mr. Shinsura entered the waiting room, and she gave him a hug. "Meet Joe and Frank Hardy."

97

The boys rose to shake hands.

"I understand that you've been trying to get to the bottom of this situation," said Tikko's father. "Made any progress?"

"We have a few ideas," said Frank. "One of them we'd like to follow up with you. It concerns the package that the sensei mailed you."

Mr. Shinsura's face took on a closed expression. "I never opened that package," he said. "My brother-in-law asked me not to—*on my honor.*" He looked at Frank. "As a student of Seino's, I'm sure you understand what that means. I'm sorry."

The Hardys were disappointed, but they respected Mr. Shinsura's promise. "Could we at least find a time to meet with you about the case?" asked Joe.

"By all means," Mr. Shinsura replied. "Why don't you drop by the dojo this evening, since I have to check on things there. We'll talk then."

The boys and Tikko agreed, and the three of them headed out to the van. "Who's up for a bite?" asked Frank.

"I could find my way around a hamburger," Tikko admitted. The three climbed into the van and headed for the Bayport Diner.

Over burgers they discussed the day's events eagerly, analyzing Frank's "fake ninja" theory, "There's got to be some sort of motive we're missing," Joe said.

"Talking of missing things," Tikko said, "do you realize that the semifinals are tomorrow?"

"Yeah—only two more days to the finals,

which should be Paul's big day," said Joe. "With the sensei flat on his back, and all those other candidates put out of commission by strange accidents, we'd better hope Paul stays in one piece till then."

The three had finished their meal and were heading out to the van. Frank and Tikko headed for the passenger doors, and Joe opened the back door of the van to climb in. "Maybe you put a scare into that ninja, today, Frank," said Joe. "If so, Paul can rest—"

Joe's voice broke off suddenly, his leg freezing in midmotion. He felt something against his ankle—something very sharp and thin.

"Joe? Are you okay?" Tikko went to put her hand on his shoulder, but Joe frantically waved her away. Slowly, he looked down to see what he'd hit with his foot. It was a trip wire—a thin piece of fishing line, stretched taut between the van door and—

With a sensation that time was moving very slowly, Joe allowed his eyes to follow the wire. It had to be attached to *something*.

When he saw what he was looking for, Joe's eyes went wide. Tucked into a corner of the van was a small, oblong object, like a little green pineapple.

Joe shouted the warning at the top of his lungs: "**GRENADE!**"

12 Adding Things Up

Frank grabbed Tikko's arm and pulled her out of the blast zone. As soon as they were out of harm's way, Joe backed off and sprinted for safety. All three hit the pavement and covered their ears, but their fears were met only with silence.

Slowly, carefully, Joe stood up and took a look at the trip wire. It was still stretched taut, still tied tightly to the ring on the grenade. But the pin was in place. He'd stopped in time before the wire ripped out the safety device and armed the bomb.

With his pocketknife Joe cut the trip wire, cautiously preserving the tension in the fishing line till he had snipped all the way through. Then, as the wire slackened, he let out a slow, deep breath.

"All set," he called to Frank and Tikko. They had stood up and were dusting off their jeans. Tikko came around to the back of the van.

"I've never actually seen a real grenade." Tikko tried to sound casual as she jammed her shaking hands into her jeans. She peered at the baseball-sized bomb, which was small enough to throw, yet big enough to have killed all of them.

"Nice save, pal," Frank said to his brother.

Joe grinned. "You can thank my sensitive ankles." He showed them the trip wire, saying, "Seems to be a lot of this going around. First Holly Stevenson, now us." He carefully wrapped the grenade in a plastic bag, hoping to preserve any fingerprints.

"Maybe we should turn that little baby over to Con Riley right now," Frank said. "I know I'd feel safer. And the sooner he gets to work on it, the better." He turned to Tikko. "Do you think your father would mind waiting a few minutes? The police station is right on the way."

After a quick search for any other surprises in the van, Joe drove to the station—extra carefully. As they walked up to Con Riley's desk the police officer looked up and smiled.

"Hello, you guys. What can I do for Bayport's finest teen sleuths today?"

"You can say hello to Tikko Shinsura," said Joe. "Mr. Watanabe's niece."

"And you can take a look at what somebody left in our van." Frank gently placed the bag with the grenade on the desk.

Con nearly jumped out of his seat. "Be careful with that!" He stared at the boys. "Give me the whole story—now."

101

Frank and Joe quickly explained what had happened, from the incident at the hospital to the booby-trapped van. "We were pretty lucky," admitted Frank.

"Luck is fine," Riley growled, throwing down the pen he'd been using to make notes. "But it helps to have numbers behind you. The hospital reported the attempt on Mr. Watanabe. I'm sure you'll be happy to hear he now has a twenty-four-hour guard in his room. And I'll have the local patrol pay special attention to the Pierson house. Now, as for you . . ."

He looked at them, then shrugged. "You know I'm going to ask you to back off this case—it's too dangerous. And we both know what happens when I tell you that—you keep on going till you solve the case. I'm going to tell you anyway. This is dangerous—*very* dangerous. So do me a favor, all of you. Be careful."

Frank and Joe looked at each other, a little embarrassed. That was exactly the advice they'd given Paul Pierson.

"Thanks, Con," Joe said. "We'll do our best."

"Just stay in one piece," Riley called after them as Tikko and the boys took their leave.

"Somebody really wants us out of the way," commented Frank as they left the police station. "It must mean we're close to something."

"Yeah—if we only could figure out what that is," Joe said.

During the drive to the dojo, they tried to fit

the pieces together, but they still couldn't come up with a picture.

They pulled up at the dojo and wandered inside. The school still had a strangely sad and deserted air without the sensei around.

In the main training room, Tikko's father stood by the wall, holding a black belt and staring at it. He seemed lost in thought. In fact, he didn't even seem to notice they were there until Tikko spoke.

"Dad!" she called excitedly. Mr. Shinsura turned around.

"Oh, hello, Tikko. Hello, Joe, Frank." Tikko's father seemed to have to pull his attention from the karate belt in his hand. "Did you kids go out to dinner?"

"Yes," said Tikko, "but we got entertainment, too." She launched into the tale of the grenade.

The more his daughter told him about the adventure, the paler Mr. Shinsura became. "Are you all right?" he asked.

"Of course, Dad."

"You could have been killed!" he said. "Having Uncle Seino in the hospital is bad enough. You're almost an adult now, not some irresponsible kid. You know well enough what I want and expect from a daughter of mine."

"But, Dad—" Tikko's own face was pale, her eyes large with hurt.

"This is a dangerous business, Tikko," he went on sternly, "and I do not want you involved." He turned and looked at the Hardys, who were

103

listening in silence. Then he spoke again to Tikko.

"And I strongly suggest that you stop spending so much time with these dangerous clowns. They'll only get you hurt—if not worse." He turned away from his daughter. "I'm going home now, Tikko. I would like you to come with me."

Mr. Shinsura stalked out of the dojo. With shoulders slumped, Tikko trailed after him.

"Whew!" said Joe.

"Come on, you dangerous clown, we've got work to do." Frank tried to keep his voice light, but he couldn't hide his anger from Joe. As they got into the van Frank slammed his door—something he never did.

Joe picked up a piece of paper from the front seat and handed it to Frank. "A love note?" he asked. "USAI PAT NO 126840987," he read aloud.

"That's the serial number from the grenade," Frank explained. "I jotted it down. Do you think it's standard military issue?"

Joe shrugged. "Who else makes grenades? The question is: where did the bad guys get it?"

"It might have been bought on the street, but when you finally look at it, there's only one place that grenade came from—the army."

Joe was skeptical. "You mean those guys held up the Pentagon?"

"No—they held up the part-time army. The National Guard. To be specific: the armories."

Joe turned to stare at his brother. "That's a big jump from one hand grenade," he said, frowning. "Or is it? Remember that traffic jam in Kingsbury? Where were all those National Guardsmen coming from?"

"The armory, I bet." Frank reached in the back of the van and grabbed the sensei's manila folder of clippings. "And where was the dojo in Redcliff?"

"Right next to the armory," both boys said at once.

Reading aloud from the folder, Frank called out: "Redcliff. Castle Hill. Kingsbury."

"The towns where karate matches were held," said Joe.

"And the towns where the armories were robbed!" said Frank. He turned over a clipping excitedly. "Look—here, on the back of this article about the karate match in Castle Hill, there's part of a story about the armory being robbed."

"A definite pattern," said Joe.

"I'll bet you anything that the sensei had picked it up," Frank said. "Since he knows the karate world so well, he must have been suspicious when the matches were won so easily—by people who weren't expected to win. Each time, a third-string substitute had to step in for the favorite. None of the people who won had to go up against anyone of their own level."

"Right. Mr. Watanabe was probably worried

about some kind of cheating going on," Joe agreed. "That's why he kept those clippings. I bet he started digging deeper."

Frank nodded. "And found that before every match—the night before—there was a robbery in an armory. The two events have to be connected somehow."

"Mr. Watanabe figured it out"—Joe looked serious—"and nearly got killed for being so smart."

"If we're right about this," said Frank, "then the armory in Riverton is about to be hit—either tonight, before the semis, or tomorrow, before the finals."

13 Stakeout

Frank picked up the mobile phone and dialed. "I'm going to tell Dad." He listened a moment, then frowned.

"Can you believe it?" he asked Joe. "The answering machine. Dad," he said a moment later. "It's Frank. Looks like our two cases are connected. We have reason to believe that the Riverton armory may be the next place the thieves will hit. I figured we should tell you, because the Riverton police might have a hard time believing us. If we get anything more, we'll let you know."

Joe stared at Frank. "So now you think we've got ninjas stealing guns."

"For the Yakuza," Frank added. "I think the time has come to try to tackle Tikko's father again. If we have it figured out right, he may change his mind about letting us know what's in that box. It could be really important."

"Good thinking," said Joe. "But I think it will work better if you talk to him alone. How about if I drop you at their house on my way to Riverton? I'd like to scope out the armory."

"A stakeout?" asked Frank.

"Well—more like a polite social visit, just to see who drops by," said Joe. "If any of our friends in ninja suits turn up, I'm sure they'll be glad to see me."

Frank and Joe drove to Tikko's house. As Frank got out he warned Joe, "Don't try to get in a fight with these guys—they know enough karate to be dangerous." He pointed to the mobile phone. "Use that to get them—call the cops."

"Gotcha," said Joe. "I'll watch out for the karate stuff. The only belts I have keep my pants up!" Grinning, he pulled away from the curb and sped off.

Frank knocked on the Shinsuras' door, and in seconds Tikko's father was there. He did not look pleased to see Frank.

"I thought I made myself clear earlier," said Mr. Shinsura. "Didn't you understand me?"

Frank felt awkward but determined. "I did understand you, sir," he said. "But my brother and I hit on an idea that may clear up all the mysterious things that have been going on. We thought it was important that you hear it. May I come in?"

Mr. Shinsura scowled but stood aside. Tikko appeared in the hallway with a nervous smile.

The three of them sat down at the kitchen table, and Frank started talking.

"Obviously," he finished up, "the sensei detected the pattern. He had been following all the matches in the other towns, and naturally he read about them in the local paper. Before long, he must have been struck by the fact that every time he read about a match, another burglary had just taken place."

"And how did these ninjas of yours find out about Seino's deduction?" asked Mr. Shinsura.

"That I don't know," replied Frank. "But I'm sure that's why he was attacked. I think we can get to the bottom of this—and find out who's behind the attacks—with your help. Mr. Watanabe must have hidden some evidence in the package that he mailed to you."

Frank and Tikko both watched Mr. Shinsura eagerly. The man's eyes were half closed as he considered Frank's words. Then, regretfully, Tikko's father shook his head.

"You're playing with something very dangerous, Frank," he said. "I'd like to help you, but I can't go back on my honor."

"Father," Tikko said, "whatever is going on here may affect Uncle Seino's honor, as well." She hesitated, then went on. "If you're trying to protect him, we know about the contract he signed with the Yakuza."

Mr. Shinsura turned away from his daughter and Frank. "I promised I wouldn't open the box unless he died. It isn't even in this house—I put it in the bank for safekeeping." He sighed. "There is so much to think of. . . ." Then he looked Frank in the eyes. "I will consider what you have proposed and meet with you tomorrow."

Mr. Shinsura rose from his chair. "I also apologize for having called you a dangerous clown," he said. "You and your brother are obviously brave and intelligent young men."

"Thank you very much, sir," Frank said.

Mr. Shinsura turned and left the room.

"You were great!" Tikko burst out. "I've never seen Dad even consider breaking a promise."

"We're still a long way from knowing what is in that package, though," Frank said. "I just hope Joe is having better luck."

At that very moment, Joe was still sitting in the van outside the Riverton armory, yawning and stretching. Usually, he had Frank to talk to on these boring jobs. Now he wished he had brought someone else along to help him stay alert. He didn't dare play the radio. He just sat and watched.

All at once, a sliver of shadow seemed to separate itself from the rest of the inky blackness around him. Then the shadow moved, becoming now darker, now paler, as it crept through the night air. Joe watched carefully and spotted two more shadows stealing through the dark.

Slowly, carefully, Joe eased the door of the van

open. Were these the dangerous ninjas who had attacked Mr. Watanabe? Or the stooges? Without a sound he got out of the van and moved to the side wall of the armory. The figures turned the corner, and Joe followed, staying about thirty yards behind. He rounded the corner just in time to see them disappearing through a window on the side of the building.

Should he go back and phone the cops now? How could only three guys loot a whole armory?

As quietly as possible, Joe followed the ninjas' path, up through the window on the side of the building. He stopped for a moment, checking out how they'd bypassed all the safeguards. Then he dropped gently down to the armory floor, allowing his eyes a few seconds to adjust to the even deeper darkness inside.

Straining eyes and ears, Joe finally detected a faint scraping noise. He tried to locate it. The sound seemed to come from down a long passageway, lit only by a dim light at the end. Joe walked down the hallway, which ended at a half-closed door. He pushed it open. There, lying on the floor, were two sentries, out cold.

Joe stepped through the door and found himself at the bottom of a spiral staircase. He climbed it quietly and emerged on a catwalk, a full story above the ground floor. He looked down.

In the dimly lighted room beneath him Joe could make out crates and boxes lining the walls. Some were marked Grenades or Rifles. Another was marked C-2 and was capable of holding enough plastic explosive to demolish a small town.

Below the catwalk, a figure dressed in black was prying up the top of a crate. Joe held his breath and peered through the dark. Something gleamed below. The ninja slid the top of the crate off. Inside, nestled cozily like breakable Christmas-tree ornaments, were half a dozen machine guns.

Joe had only a second to wonder where the man's two accomplices were. Suddenly a shadow fell across his line of vision, and he looked up and saw another ninja swinging down toward him from the rafters above.

Joe took a step backward, only to feel a hard forearm wrap itself around his throat.

14 Without a Trace

Joe didn't hesitate. He rammed an elbow back into his attacker's stomach while raking a heel down the ninja's shin. It might not have been karate, but it worked. The hold on him loosened.

Grabbing the banister of the catwalk, Joe vaulted over, swung briefly, and began to use the struts like monkey bars to cross the floor below. In a moment he was directly above a tall crate. He dropped onto it, then jumped from there to the floor.

The ninja who had been opening the boxes headed straight for him, the crowbar still in his hands. Joe grabbed a long plank from one of the crates and swung hard, knocking the tool from the ninja's grasp. Even without a weapon, the ninja charged. Joe grabbed a box of loose bullets and spilled them out on the floor. In midstride the ninja slipped, flew a few feet into the air, and landed on his back.

113

Joe turned quickly as, with a clatter, the remaining two attackers descended the stairs. They were headed straight for him.

Joe looked wildly around. There was a large electric forklift truck right behind him. He leaped on, pressing buttons at random.

The engine started with an enormous groan and roar. Steering the huge machine awkwardly, Joe headed straight for the attacking ninjas, who nearly fell over themselves to get out of his way.

Suddenly, although not a word was spoken, a message seemed to pass among the ninjas. Joe watched as all three quickly and silently retreated, seeming to melt into the shadows.

He looked around in surprise. Then he saw the reason for the hasty departure. The door near the spiral staircase was open, and there, with guns at the ready, stood two more army guards. One of the men pursued the retreating ninjas; the other trained his gun on Joe.

Joe took a deep breath and shut off the engine of the forklift.

"Boy, am I—"

"Hands in the air," ordered the guard. "And don't talk."

Joe shrugged and did as he was told. Okay, the guard hadn't recognized him as a hero. But he had saved him from a three-on-one fight. The guard motioned for Joe to come down. Joe stepped down slowly and carefully from the machine, with his hands over his head. Then the guard unhooked the handcuffs from his belt and spun Joe around, cuffing Joe's hands behind his back and marching him unceremoniously down the hall to the security room.

The door opened and the other guard came in. "The others got clean away," he said, "but this time they didn't get any weapons."

"At least we caught this one," said his partner. "I'm going to call the authorities."

Before he was halfway through dialing, however, the authorities arrived.

The guards sprang to their feet as Fenton Hardy strode in, accompanied by a uniformed army officer.

"Good evening," Fenton said to the guards. Then he looked at his son. "Hello, Joe. Are you here as reinforcements or as a burglar?"

Joe smiled ruefully.

"You know this kid, Mr. Hardy?" asked the young sentry, trying to get his rifle back over his shoulder.

"He's my son," said the detective. "And I'm pretty sure I know why he was here. Did you explain to the guards, Joe?"

"I hadn't actually gotten around to it," said Joe, with the shadow of a wink at his father. Fenton Hardy appeared to understand, because he winked back.

"Okay," said Fenton, "let's hear what happened here tonight. But first, a word of explanation for Colonel Kelsey of army intelligence here." He turned to the officer. "My boys, Frank and Joe, are actually fairly well known in these parts for their work as amateur detectives."

"I'm aware of it, Fenton," responded the army man. "That's the kind of thing we're expected to know in the intelligence branch. Joe?"

Thus encouraged, Joe told his story. Most of it seemed to leave the guards in some confusion. "They were dressed in black, that's for sure," the one who caught Joe agreed.

"But I thought ninjas were just something in the movies," his partner said.

Things were soon straightened out at the armory. With an apology to the guards for the disturbance, the Hardys and Colonel Kelsey left.

Outside, the parking lot was crawling with FBI agents, checking for clues. Colonel Kelsey turned to Joe.

"Well," he said, "you certainly have had an exciting evening. Imagine the coincidence! For a minute there, I thought we had our armory burglars. This crew was good, but I think they were only pulling a copycat crime. Good work, though, Joe."

He called to the FBI men, telling them to clear out, then turned to Mr. Hardy. "Coming, Fenton?"

"I think I'll ride back with Joe," said the detective. "I'll be in touch in the morning."

The Hardys, father and son, climbed in the van. As soon as the other men were out of earshot Joe burst out, "Coincidences! Copycat!" Joe looked at his father. "You don't buy that, do you, Dad?"

"No, I don't think I do. It's pretty unlikely that there would be two groups of people skillful enough to pull off these robberies—or as foolhardy. Nearly as foolhardy as you were." He gave his son a look that turned into a headshake.

"I think you've stumbled on to something really crucial here. But I'm working for the army in this case—for Colonel Kelsey, in fact."

"So what? You're the detective, not Colonel Kelsey. Why don't they ask what you think?"

"Because Colonel Kelsey is more interested in what his *boss* thinks, and the general would like to believe that these crimes are being committed by terrorists." Fenton Hardy shook his head. "Even if there's no proof. So we've wasted time checking out half the malcontents in creation."

"Sounds like your hands are tied, Dad," said Joe.

"They were—until now. You've given me a whole new line to explore."

Joe beamed at his father. "We'll be extra careful on our case, Dad, I promise. And we'll keep you up to date, if we find anything that can help you."

"If you want to help me, just make sure Colonel Kelsey is on hand for any future 'coincidences,'" Fenton Hardy said.

Over breakfast the next day, Joe, Frank, and their father discussed the case more fully. Frank, of course, was eager for every detail of the previous night's adventures.

When Joe told how Colonel Kelsey had managed to ignore all the facts, Frank couldn't help laughing.

"Did you keep a straight face, Joe?" he asked.

"As long as I could," said Joe.

Their father spoke. "I've told Joe that I'm very proud of your work so far," he said. "You've given us a whole new direction to explore—if I can convince the powers-that-be. I just ask two things —if you're going to keep on your case, be careful. And—since it looks like we are working on the same case here—I want you to keep me informed."

"Will do, Dad," said Frank. "By the way, Joe—we had a call last night from Charles Harris."

"The retired fellow who collects typefaces?" asked Fenton Hardy.

"Yes—we asked him to analyze the anonymous letter that was sent to Paul," responded Joe. He turned to Frank. "Any leads?"

The elder brother shook his head. "Maybe. He says the letters were mainly from local newspapers—and a magazine on martial arts."

"So it's from somebody nearby who's into karate." Joe shrugged. "We kind of knew that from the message."

"You'll find a lead soon enough, boys, I'm sure," said their father. "And when you do, remember—keep me informed."

"You've got it, Dad," Frank promised. He was glad his father trusted them on this case.

"And, Dad," said Joe, "thanks again for coming to the rescue."

"You can show your thanks," Fenton Hardy said, rising from the table. "It's your turn to do the breakfast dishes."

As Joe washed and Frank dried they laid out their plans for the day.

"Before we drive over to the Riverton Civic Arena for the semifinals, I want to stop off at the *Bayport Times*," Frank said.

"Checking in with Jim Lao again—good idea," Joe said. "After hearing about the Yakuza, I'll bet he's been doing a little digging."

When Frank and Joe had finished cleaning up, they drove downtown to the crowded city room. Jim Lao greeted them cheerfully. "I was hoping you guys would show up," he said. "You promised me a scoop on this Yakuza thing."

"We're still working on it," said Frank. "Actually, we came back to pick your brain. Have you picked up any more information?"

"Nothing concrete. After you left the other day I decided to check around. All I met with was a very stony silence—even from my usually talkative sources. That must mean something is up."

"Any leads?" asked Joe.

"One of my contacts did agree to talk," said Lao. "But when I met with him he was obviously frightened. He told me that there's a major war going on among the Yakuza back home. Different

119

clans are struggling for control. And, he said, it's not like the usual Yakuza war—swords and light guns. We're talking major firepower."

The boys were thoughtful. "I think that information fits in with the bits and pieces we've got," said Frank.

"So when do I get my scoop?" countered the reporter.

Frank chuckled. "Sorry, not yet. But you'll hear the news first—as soon as we finally get the pieces together."

The boys took their leave. It was nearly time for the semifinals to start. Even though they were sure that Paul would make it to the finals tomorrow, the Hardys didn't want to miss a minute of the matches. They were also worried over the mysterious accidents that had taken place in Kingsbury and Redcliff. Even though Paul had left with a protective group of students from the dojo, the Hardys wanted to keep a personal eye on him.

Frank and Joe made good time on the drive to Riverton. They pulled the van into the parking lot at the big civic arena where the matches were being held and parked. But when they came in the entrance, Frank and Joe stopped dead.

Right ahead of them stood a figure in a black gi.

"A ninja?" Frank whispered. He and Joe split up to come in on either side of the figure. The guy's face was covered—in a hockey mask! The Hardys moved in, each grabbing an arm.

"What are you guys doing?" The "ninja" tore loose, removing his mask to reveal an angry face.

"Why are you wearing that outfit?" Frank demanded.

"What's wrong with it? Nothing against it in the rules." The guy straightened his black gi.

The Hardys realized they had gathered a crowd, including several other competitors. They saw what the "ninja" meant. Several other people wore black gis. One guy had a karate outfit in a camouflage pattern.

"Sorry," Joe apologized. "We thought you were someone else." They hurried off toward the locker room. "Can't take you anywhere," Joe jokingly complained.

Frank grinned. "It's my first big competition—how was I to know?" His smile faded. "Too bad the sensei can't be here," said Frank.

"We'll give him the blow-by-blow when he gets better," Joe promised.

"Speaking of which—" Frank pointed. "There's our own sports reporter." Frank's classmate and fellow karate student, Billy Brown, stood in the hallway to the lockers. He had a video recorder under one arm and a mike under the other.

"Hullo, Hardys," said Billy.

"Billy, what do you think about today's judges?" asked Frank. "Will they keep an eye on Keith? Or will they let him fight dirty?"

"They're going to try to be objective. Me—I'm

going to get it all on tape, so we can resolve disputes with instant replay."

"Great idea!" said Joe, and Frank agreed. If Keith tried anything, he'd be caught in living color.

"Have you seen Paul?" asked Frank.

"He was headed for the lockers a while ago," said Billy.

The Hardys thanked Billy and continued that way themselves.

They opened the door to the locker room and called Paul's name. Silence. Frank moved to the next aisle, where he saw a pile of clothes on the floor—including a sweatshirt that he recognized as Paul's.

"Pierson!" Frank shouted more sharply.

"Hey, Frank, listen!" cried Joe. The boys heard the clash of metal garbage cans being knocked to the ground and a muffled groan.

"This way!" shouted Frank, heading for the fire exit. He crashed through the door with his shoulder, Joe right behind him. The area beyond the locker room was empty. But about twenty yards away was a big garbage dumpster, and just on the other side of that was a dented black van.

Headed straight for the van, moving swiftly, were two tall figures dressed in black. Between them they half carried, half dragged a white-clad person, bound hand and foot. Paul Pierson!

"Paul!" yelled Frank. The Hardys made a dash for it—but the ninjas were surprisingly fast, even with their wriggling burden.

In two strides they reached the back of the van, tossed Paul in, and climbed aboard. Before the door closed the engine roared.

Frank had almost reached the doors when the van took off, tires squealing.

Paul was gone!

15 "In This Corner..."

"See which way they go! I'll get our van!" shouted Joe, tearing along a connecting alley to the parking lot. Frank raced to the end of the alley to watch as the ninjas' van made a left, then a quick right. Then Joe pulled up, and Frank leaped into their van.

"They turned right onto McGeorge Avenue," said Frank. "Go!"

Joe grabbed the stick shift and, gears whining, they took off. Around the corner they found the black van, way ahead of them. With a screech of tires, it took another left.

The Hardys continued on for three blocks, cutting the ninjas' lead on the straightaway. The black van made a right this time, darting down a narrow street. The Hardys came around the corner just in time to see the van jockey its way around a loading dock. Then a truck moved out to block the road.

"Back it up, Joe," Frank ordered. "I think they're headed for Elmhurst Road," he said. "Let's try another route to cut them off."

Joe jolted into reverse, cleared the corner, then took the van down two blocks at top speed. They made a right onto an old cobblestone street. "Nobody takes this road—so no traffic," Joe explained as they bounced along.

They reached the corner just as the van crossed their path.

They'd already started turning in pursuit when a passenger car came barreling through the intersection, horn blaring. Joe had to swerve to miss it. Just in time!

"Whew," he said.

"They're making a left up ahead—looks like Ridgeway Street," said Frank.

"They won't get through," said Joe. "It was on the news last night—a big water-main break. The street's dug up from end to end."

"Then we've got 'em," said Frank.

Seconds later the Hardys turned left onto Ridgeway Street. There, as Joe had said, was a giant hole in the ground with all kinds of excavating equipment. And parked right in the middle was a dented black van.

The Hardys screeched to a halt and jumped out. "No sign of anyone around," Joe said. "Those ninjas have pulled their usual miracle-disappearance act."

"But did they take Paul with them?" Frank asked.

As if in answer, a loud thumping on the van door came from within. A trick? Frank opened the door cautiously. There was Paul, bound and gagged.

Joe quickly untied Paul, and Frank removed the gag. "Thanks," the karate champ gasped.

"You okay?" Frank asked.

"Yeah. You guys are the greatest. But I've got to get back. I'm due to fight in a few minutes."

"Hang on, champ," said Frank. "Maybe we'd better file a report with the police."

"Can't that wait?" asked Paul. "If they take my statement now, I'll miss the match. They'll want me to talk to them all day."

The Hardys couldn't deny that Paul had a point.

"Okay," said Frank. "We'll hold off. In fact, if we can supply them with a connection between the rigged matches and the burglaries, everyone will be in better shape."

"What connection?" asked Paul.

"Later." Joe grinned. "Let's hustle."

· They headed back to the arena. On the way, Frank phoned Con Riley with the license number of the black van to see if it could be traced. The police officer promised to call the Hardys later with the results.

When they reached the arena, they spotted Tikko standing by the entrance.

"Where have you guys been?" she asked impatiently. She glanced curiously at Paul, who was dusting off his gi and rearranging his belt.

"I went for a ride," said Paul.

Tikko gave him a frustrated look. "Go pick on Keith Owen," she said. "I need to talk to these guys."

With a smile, Paul headed off to the contestants' lockers. Tikko turned to the Hardys.

"My father opened the box," she said.

"And?" asked the boys in unison.

Tikko looked upset. "And *nothing!* He won't tell me what's in there."

She shook her head. "When I came down to breakfast this morning, Dad was already at the table—staring at the box. He'd gotten it out of the bank first thing."

"And then?" Joe asked.

"He said, 'Tikko, do you trust those boys?'" She looked at Frank and Joe. "I said I did. Then my father took a knife and broke a red wax seal at one end of the box. It held together a silk wrapping. When that fell away, Dad lifted the lid."

She stamped in frustration. "Before I could cross the room and take a look inside, he'd closed the box, grabbed up the whole bundle, and stormed out."

"Was he angry at you for taking a peek?" Joe asked.

"Or maybe it was what he saw in the box," Frank said thoughtfully. "We'll talk to him later. He must have had a good reason for such a strong reaction."

"Frank's right," said Joe. "Let's go in and see if

Paul's experience has made him ready to do battle."

Tikko handed each of the boys a ticket. The Hardys took them and headed once more to the locker room, where they found Paul doing some breathing exercises.

They also found Keith Owen changing into his gi. "I'm sure surprised to see you here, chump," he said to Paul. "I didn't think you'd have the nerve to show—"

Frank cut him off. "I thought you'd be exercising your lungs, not your mouth, Owen."

"Hey, it's the Two Stooges." Keith grinned mockingly. "Coming here to help poor Paulie? He hasn't got a chance. Even if his teacher wasn't a wimp, he wouldn't have had a chance." Keith sat down on the bench to remove his sneakers. "But as things stand now—without his sensei as his good-luck charm, this guy is dead in the water."

"I'd say *you're* the one who needs help," said Frank. "You haven't got a bunch of your buddies lined up as judges. So you've got a problem— you'll have to fight fair."

"Whoooaah! I'm real scared!" said Keith. But he backed off and turned to finish dressing.

Keith had left his sneakers next to Joe, on the bench. Joe picked up one of the shoes, ready to throw it across the locker room at Keith, when he noticed something—black stains on the soles.

Stepping so his body hid the sneakers from Keith, Joe took a closer look at the shoe. The tread—a pattern of circles and dots—looked familiar. *Very* familiar. It was the same pattern he'd seen on the rooftop the day he and Frank chased the archer.

Looking closer at the black stains, Joe nodded. Tar! And between the dots and circles, very faint, was a yellow smudge or two. Paint!

Joe turned to stare at Keith Owen, shrugging into his gi. Had he really fired the arrow at Paul and sent Holly Stevenson falling down those stairs?

Could Keith really be a ninja warrior—a Shadow Killer?

16 Back to the Warehouse

Quickly handing Frank the sneaker, Joe whispered, "Take a look!"

Frank examined the tread and realized immediately what the stains meant. He casually put the sneaker back on the bench. Then he said, "Come on, you guys. Looks like Paul is ready for today's round."

"Ladies and gentlemen—in that corner, the Wimp," said Keith, with his usual nasty tone. The three boys ignored Keith's remark and headed out to the arena. As Frank passed, Keith said, "When I'm finished wiping out your buddy, it's going to be your turn, chump."

Frank turned and stared straight at Keith. "You've got a spot on your gi," he said, pointing at Keith's chest. Keith looked down, and Frank abruptly flicked his finger upward, catching the tip of Keith's nose. As Keith's face reddened with fury Frank backed out of the locker room fast. "Mr. Watanabe taught me that move—the Iron Finger Flick."

"Your turn is coming, chump!" Keith shouted after Frank.

Out in the arena, Paul and Joe were laughing so hard they almost were out of breath. "Usually, I don't like to do that kind of stuff," said Frank, catching up with them and laughing himself. "But he really deserved it."

"He was so busy being nasty, he fell for one of the oldest tricks in the book." Paul turned to the Hardys. "Well, wish me luck." He headed off to join the other contestants.

As the boys watched him go they grew serious again. "I think we have what we need to sew this one up," said Joe.

"Except hard evidence," said Frank. "We know Keith shot that arrow at us—the stains on his sneakers were definitely tar, and the tread will match the prints up there. But that's the only real proof we have."

Joe nodded. "So, dressed as a ninja, Keith has been trying to keep Paul out of the match. Do you think he's connected with the armory break-ins, too? He must be—since all the burglaries in the other towns appear to be somehow linked with the karate matches there."

"Plus—you saw the ninjas at the Riverton armory. There must be a tie-in," Frank pointed out. "But we need more than a 'there must' to go on." Frank spotted Keith in the crowd. "Who are those guys he's talking to? They seem pretty chummy."

Joe looked across the arena to see Keith in angry conversation with two other kids. "Let's ask Brown," he said. "Hey, Billy!" he called to the young would-be sportscaster. Billy Brown looked up briefly from his video camera, then came to join the Hardys.

"Who are those guys with Keith?" asked Joe.

Billy looked across the arena. "Ray Norton and Dick Blake," he said. "The winners from the Redcliff and Kingsbury matches." He shouldered his camera and shot a few seconds of tape, speaking into the mike. "Locally favored to come in second, privately favored to break his neck, is Keith Owen—seen here chatting with two others who should never have made it this far."

Joe and Frank looked at each other, each thinking the same thing. Two buddies—two ninjas who tried to kidnap Paul. Two competitors who had won their championships because of "accidents" the other contestants had suffered. And Keith Owen's footprint had turned up where Dick Blake's opponent had fallen down the stairs. Clearly the Hardys were not being overimaginative. Conspiracy was at work here.

Billy Brown wandered away to shoot more prematch footage. Joe turned to Frank. "Those three are fixing the matches," he said.

"But where do the Yakuza fit in?" Frank asked. "And who attacked Mr. Watanabe?"

"It's almost like we have two separate cases," Joe agreed. "The big question is why? It seems like a lot of work to make sure your buddies get a trip to Japan."

A bell sounded, and the contestants all assembled on the mats set up on the arena floor. The Hardys joined Tikko at the sidelines. They watched, totally absorbed, as the semifinalists performed a series of katas, or exercises, first as a group, then solo.

Although the movements in each exercise were all the same—set by tradition—the Hardys and Tikko were struck by the different degrees of talent on display. Even Joe, who knew very little about karate, could see that Keith and Paul were by far the best.

Then the time came for the exercises done with just one partner. Again, some of the movements were set, but Joe was amazed at the agility required to carry them out. It was like watching some sort of dance—a deadly dance, if some of those movements became blows. Paul was partnered with another brown belt, instead of fighting Keith today. The judges must have been sure that he would have to go up against Keith in the finals tomorrow, reflected Frank.

When the judges finally announced the scores, no one was surprised. Keith and Paul had the most points and were slated to go head to head the next morning, in the finals.

After the matches, the Hardys and Tikko fought their way through the crowd to the locker room, where they met Paul. The four kids joined the others still streaming out of the civic arena and into the packed parking lot.

"I'll go check in with the police, the way I promised I would," said Paul. "Now that the semis are over, they're welcome to their report."

"Can we give you a lift, Tikko?" asked Frank.

"Sure—wherever you guys are headed." She grinned as she climbed in.

"See you, Paul," called Joe. "We'll touch base later."

They were still stuck in traffic when the phone rang. Frank picked it up. "Hello?"

"Con Riley, here. I thought I might find you boys on the road. Look, we've traced the vehicle for you. Easy enough—it was reported stolen right after you called."

Frank felt a little disappointed—another lead up in smoke. "Where'd it come from?"

"It's a van registered to a company called Oteman, Inc. Maybe you know of them."

"Oh, I know them all right," said Frank. "Thanks a million." He hung up and told Joe and Tikko the news.

"Oteman?" Tikko said.

Frank nodded. "They reported the van as stolen—right *after* the ninjas had to bail out and leave it. What does that make you think?"

"Makes me think that nice Mr. Tanaka is in this scam up to his neck," Joe said. "I vote for a little patrol action."

"Me, too," Tikko agreed. "What's the plan?"

"Tikko, I seem to recall that your father wasn't too wild about you hanging out with us since we might be heading for trouble."

"Well, I'm *already* in trouble," she retorted. "My uncle is in a coma, my father is freaking out, and it seems like every time I turn around someone is being kidnapped or threatened. Besides," she added, "you guys don't know how to throw a shuriken. If you bring me, I promise to teach you how."

The Hardys looked at her, trying to keep their faces straight.

Finally, Joe grinned. "It's okay by me," he said. "So far Tikko has been able to handle everything that's come at us."

"I can see when I'm outvoted," said Frank. "First we have some dinner, then we visit Oteman."

They stopped at a nearby restaurant and ate lightly. When they had finished, Tikko suggested that they stop off at her house. "I've got some stuff to pick up," she said.

Frank took the wheel and drove them to Tikko's. She ran into her house and came back out a few moments later. When Tikko joined them in the van, she was dressed all in black, with a black baseball cap jammed down on her head. Her trusty leather bag was over her shoulder. At her belt were two shurikens.

"Ready for action?" asked Joe.

"You bet," she replied. Frank put the van in gear and headed for the Oteman warehouse.

As they drove, Tikko and the Hardys put together what they remembered of the Oteman grounds. Tikko looked at her watch. "We should get there just as darkness falls," she said. "That should help."

"We'll still need to scout the place before we try getting in," Joe said. "I remember seeing lots of guards on the way in."

By now, Frank had brought them to the top of a hill overlooking Oteman headquarters. The entire complex was enclosed by an eight-foot fence with barbed wire on the top. Bright lights shone all along the boundary. From where they stood they could see three gates. Each gate had a guard post with two guards. More security people patrolled the grounds.

"Somehow, it looks scarier at night," Tikko said quietly.

"But there is a way in," Frank said. "I noticed when we were here before that trucks pull right up to the big loading bays. Our best bet is to sneak onto a truck before it goes through the gate, and then we can jump off right into the warehouse through the loading bay."

Joe and Tikko agreed. They left the van where it was and headed down to the road for the last turn before the truckers' gate. Twice they had to dodge the headlights of cars as they moved.

But once they were in position, they didn't have to wait long. The first vehicle that came through was a regular panel truck, but the back door was closed, so they couldn't sneak aboard.

But in a few more minutes another truck approached—this one a large flatbed rig, with just a few boxes and an old tarp on the cargo bed.

"This is it!" whispered Frank. While the driver waited for the guard to open the gate, the Hardys and Tikko swung up quietly onto the truck bed and quickly crept under the tarp.

The truck rumbled through the gate, up to the dock. Then it backed up to one of the big loading bays. Tikko and the boys waited silently until the driver cut the engine and got out.

"I want to see the night foreman about the last shipment," they heard him say. "I think I got shortchanged. *Then* we load." Footsteps moved away as another voice said, "Okay."

"Now!" whispered Joe.

He, Frank, and Tikko slid out from under the tarp, darted across the loading dock, and made a dash for the huge warehouse.

The place was even more eerie at night than it had been in the afternoon light. Just a few lights glimmered over the exit doors. Everywhere else was in darkness. Huge crates stood like small, silent mountains.

Frank gestured for Joe and Tikko to follow him. He stole over to one unsealed crate, marked Damaged in Transit. Return to Maker.

"This is what I'm curious about," Frank whispered. "Last time we were here, I noticed a lot of damaged goods going back to Japan. An awful lot, for a successful import/export business."

He crouched over the crate and began to pry

up a plank, then reached inside and pulled out a box marked Cassette Tapes. He opened it.

The top layer was cassette tapes, all right. But beneath that, nestled carefully in the box, were half a dozen army-issue hand grenades.

"Smuggler's trick," Joe said. "Just like Jim Lao told us." He pulled more boxes from the crate, including one marked AM/FM Radios. Joe opened it—to find a thousand rounds of ammunition.

"This is the missing link," whispered Frank in satisfaction. "Tanaka is ripping off the armories and smuggling the weapons out of the country. *He* must be our Yakuza connection."

"And somehow the crooked karate students are working for him," mused Joe. "That's why the matches are fixed."

Suddenly brilliant light flooded the area they were standing in. The Hardys and Tikko were momentarily blinded. They could hear footsteps rushing toward them.

"Uh, Frank," Joe said. "I think they may have noticed us."

Tikko's voice was equally tight. "And I don't think that's the welcome committee coming our way."

17 Yakuza!

"Very good indeed," a voice drawled from behind the blinding lights. The Hardys and Tikko all recognized the voice, and it sent a chill of the bleakest fear through them. As the other lights in the warehouse came up, their eyes slowly cleared, and they saw that they were surrounded.

Mr. Tanaka stood before them. From out of the shadows—dressed, of course as ninjas—came Keith Owen, Dick Blake, and Ray Norton. Off to both sides were a few large, tough-looking men —Mr. Tanaka's warehouse employees.

Frank and Joe had been in sticky situations like this one before. They didn't even need to communicate. But Tikko was new to all this. Joe could feel her tensing beside him. To yell? To attack? He knew this—it was the wrong time. They still had to assess the danger and pick their moment for a break. Silently, Joe grabbed her hand and squeezed. Tikko got the message.

"So, we were right," Frank said. "You are Yakuza."

"Yes, my young friend. Although how you of all people"—he made a gesture that included Joe and Tikko—"should have discovered my secret . . . Well, life is full of surprises, and not all of them pleasant ones."

"Kinshasu clan," said Joe.

Mr. Tanaka looked at him in surprise. "My, you certainly have done your homework. Yes. I am the chief of Kinshasu. For all the good that knowledge will do you now." He gave them a thin-lipped smile. If the Hardys hadn't known better, they'd have thought Tanaka was actually sad at the prospect of killing them.

"And you're fighting with the other clans," Tikko added.

Mr. Tanaka bowed to her. "Indeed, Miss Shinsura, you are correct. My clan is engaged in a bloody civil war with our fellow Yakuza. The other clans foolishly wish to take a share of our smuggling operations. We cannot allow that. So"—he shrugged his shoulders and raised his hands in a gesture of helplessness—"we use our smuggling skills to make sure that no one takes over our part of the business."

He looked around at the faces of his captives. At this moment he looked like a professor, delivering a favorite lecture.

Then Tanaka's smile became wolfish. "You may know the saying Victory goes to the side with the most guns. Your country's armories have provided my clan with more than enough guns for victory."

"You've got big plans," Joe told him.

"Very big," Tanaka agreed. "Not just for our business holdings in this country, but for our *people.* I've been working to recruit Americans, but a problem arose. The philosophy of our little group is hard for Americans to understand. They must have in-depth training. But how to bring the recruits to Japan for that training without raising suspicions? A true problem."

"So you hit on the idea of sponsoring a karate tour," suggested Frank, "and recruiting junior thugs from within the dojos."

"Precisely," said Mr. Tanaka. "And when the recruits return from their tour, they will be true Yakuza. I will provide them with suitable jobs in the major port cities in this country. And Kinshasu will remain the leading Yakuza clan."

"Big business, indeed," said Frank. "I'm impressed how your clan has kept up with the times—even if it means giving up old traditions."

"What do you mean?" Mr. Tanaka demanded.

"Well—I thought the Yakuza was an honorable outfit—among criminals, that is. I must have been wrong."

Mr. Tanaka looked deeply offended. "Honor is everything to us," he said.

"Then why did you recruit this lowlife?" asked Frank, gesturing at Keith Owen. "He knows nothing about honor. He can't even spell the word."

Keith took a menacing step forward, but Tanaka stopped him with a look.

"Mr. Owen has been useful to us," Mr. Tanaka answered blandly. "In spite of his occasional crudeness." The wolf look came back for a moment. "If his crudeness gets in our way, that will be the end of him—and it."

Keith looked appalled but said nothing.

"Now, the Hardys would be even more useful," said Mr. Tanaka with a greedy gleam in his eye. "It is a pity that you won't be corrupted. You could bring us so much."

"Enough of this," Tikko put in abruptly. Mr. Tanaka looked at her in surprise—he'd been completely ignoring her. "I demand to know why you tried to kill my uncle," Tikko went on. He's a great man and a great sensei. *He* understands Honor." She gave Tanaka a challenging look.

"Oh, but you have hit on the point exactly, Tikko. It *was* a point of honor. The repayment of a debt, if you will. You see, many years ago, your uncle was helpful to us. Not one of us, precisely, but he was helpful. At the time, he desperately needed money, and he didn't seem to care where it came from.

"We needed a sensei, so I hired Watanabe. Only when he discovered he was teaching ninjas did he become uneasy about his new employer.

"One day his suspicions were confirmed. He

142

declared that he wished to terminate our arrangement. But he was too good for us to let him go. We tried to persuade him gently that resigning was a bad idea, for *him*. We used quiet methods to show him the wisdom of helping us. He signed a contract. Still he tried to leave us. We were forced to try more forcefully to get him to stay. . . ." Tanaka's voice trailed off.

"You burned down his house!" cried Tikko.

"Well, as I say, we worked hard to persuade him. No luck, I'm afraid. Now, many years later, I have attempted once more to enlist his talents. But he has declined."

"So *you* beat him up?" asked Joe.

Mr. Tanaka looked surprised. "I merely made sure he was unconscious. My young friend here was overzealous," he said, indicating Keith. "I only wanted to scare the sensei, not to kill him. His loss would be tremendously sad." Tanaka actually managed to *look* sad.

He shook his head, turning away from Tikko and the Hardys. "The story is now ended." Tanaka motioned to the waiting ninjas. "If you please," he said to Keith and the other karate students. "There is work to be done here."

Then he strode off into the office area.

Keith, with a look of cruel anticipation in his eyes, began to move in on Frank. Between the karate crew and their hulking pals, things looked pretty grim.

But the Hardys weren't standing around to get

143

mobbed. Joe leaped to the attack, charging one of Tanaka's men, knocking him to the ground and breaking the threatening circle.

In the momentary confusion that followed, Tikko and Frank moved with lightning speed. Tikko let a shuriken fly, catching one of Tanaka's men in the back of the leg and bringing him to his knees in pain. She spun the other knife at Keith, who managed to dodge it, but the diversion gave Frank the extra split second he needed to prepare for Keith's attack.

The rest of Keith's troops were breaking up. Joe had made a successful run for it and was leading Ray Norton on a desperate chase through the mazes of crates and boxes awaiting shipment. Tikko also darted suddenly away, with Dick Blake in pursuit. She scrambled nimbly up a stack of boxes and leaped from one stack to the next and the next, before jumping down into the network of aisles crisscrossing the huge warehouse.

Tikko and Joe both headed for the nearest exit. Frank, however, had to face Keith. He retreated behind the crate they'd opened only minutes before.

Keith sneered, advancing with his hands like blades. "You don't think hiding will help you?"

Frank shrugged. "If I can't win with karate, I'll need another sport." His hand darted into the box marked Cassettes, coming out with one of the hand grenades. Then a quick windup sent the grenade flying at fastball speed, straight at Keith!

The ninja-in-training committed the cardinal error of karate—he flinched. His block was a split second too late. The grenade caught him in the shoulder, staggering him.

Frank was already vaulting over the box as the grenade bounced to the floor, harmless. He had never pulled the arming pin. Whipping past Keith, he took him down with a swift kick. Then he set off after Joe and Tikko, running faster than he'd ever known his legs would carry him. The three converged, racing breathlessly down the long final stretch toward a door marked Exit.

Suddenly, less than ten yards ahead of them, Mr. Tanaka stepped out from between two large crates. Directly behind him were Ray Norton and Dick Blake; racing madly at them from behind was Keith Owen.

"Go for it!" shouted Frank, with all his might. The three of them tried to charge Mr. Tanaka and his forces, but the executive astounded them by executing a series of lightning-fast kicks and chops. His hands sliced the air with razor precision; his feet seemed to fly everywhere, hardly touching the ground.

As he whirled and kicked, his minions advanced behind him, producing samurai swords. Then, with a final series of whirling kicks, Mr. Tanaka produced a pair of *nun-chakas*—Japanese fighting sticks—as if from thin air.

The escape route before them was solidly blocked. Behind them advanced Keith Owen, who now also had a sword. On each side they were walled in by a high, insurmountable stack of cargo containers.

The Hardys and Tikko slowed their charge.

Working together, they'd broken the last circle of death.

But trapped in this alley, they had no hope against the enemy's odds.

18 The Finals

Mr. Tanaka advanced on the Hardys and Tikko, brandishing the deadly nun-chakas, twirling them in his hands and smiling a slow smile of satisfaction. Frank felt a rough kick from behind and knew that Keith Owen was there, just waiting for the signal to move in for the kill.

All at once Frank and Joe became aware of a hushed, scurrying noise. Mr. Tanaka must have heard it, too, for he turned and peered behind him. Nothing.

Then a fierce scream shattered the stillness of the standoff. "HIeeeeeYAH!" Frank and Joe looked up to see a half-dozen karate students, led by Paul Pierson, jump down from atop the stacks of boxes.

Paul took on Ray Norton and Dick Blake at once, sending them crashing along the floor with a series of laser-fast kicks. Tikko turned on one of Tanaka's men, dealing him a swift and surprising kick to the jaw, followed by a fast chop to the neck.

Frank whipped around on Keith Owen, who was still trying to take in the new turn of events. A straight right to the jaw sent Keith to the ground. Frank knew that Keith was more than a match for him in karate, so he took care to wind Keith up with a few good old-fashioned kidney punches.

Joe stepped in as one of Tanaka's guards was advancing on Frank from the rear, samurai sword at the ready. A football tackle took the guard into one of the mountainous crates, putting him out of commission.

Mr. Tanaka had seen his forces crumbling before the surprise attack. Now he leaped to the attack, twirling the nun-chakas to nail three students in one move. Suddenly a quiet, determined voice penetrated the commotion of the fight.

"Tanaka-san," said the voice. "Leave the students alone. *I* challenge you. In the name of honor." Out of the shadows stepped Mr. Shinsura, dressed in a gi, with a black belt at his waist.

By now the kids—with the help of Paul Pierson and the karate students—had Mr. Tanaka's thugs sewn up. Paul and the other students bound Tanaka's men with their karate belts and stood back to watch the fight between the two older men.

Tanaka leaped for Mr. Shinsura, his nun-chakas whizzing. He swung for the head as his opponent ducked. The weapon smashed in the side of a crate. A couple of stolen rifles dropped out onto the floor. With a dazzling roll, Mr. Shinsura came under Tanaka's next attack, grabbing one of the empty guns. In two short strokes with his new weapon, he knocked the nun-chakas from Mr. Tanaka's hands.

"Now we are matched for a fight," said Mr. Shinsura, tossing away the battered gun.

"Hieeeyah!" he shouted. In a burst of speed, he was in the air, with both feet off the ground. Then with blinding swiftness he delivered two kicks in succession, knocking Mr. Tanaka to the ground.

Tanaka came up, charging Mr. Shinsura. His hands stabbed, his fists punched, he kicked in deadly combinations. But for all that, Tanaka's viciousness was no match for the power of the anger unleashed in Tikko's father.

Mr. Shinsura blocked and parried every blow, until he grabbed Tanaka by the arm and flipped him onto the floor, where he landed with a sickening thud. As abruptly as it had begun, the fight was over.

"Now honor is restored," said Tikko's father. He bowed to his defeated opponent, who lay dazed on the hard cement floor.

The Hardys and Tikko became aware of the sound of approaching police sirens. The three of them had never been so glad to hear that sound before.

In moments, the warehouse was swarming with

police, FBI, and army intelligence officers. Fenton Hardy was there, along with Colonel Kelsey. Other senior members of Mr. Hardy's task force directed the roundup. Before tending to business, the famous detective strode over to where his sons stood and shook them by the hand.

"Copycat crime, eh, Joe?" Fenton Hardy laughed. "You boys have shown that there's more than one way to skin a Yakuza!"

The Hardys and Tikko soon had the full story of their rescue, too.

"Tikko's father came looking for you at the dojo," Paul explained. "I'd made my police report and was there training for tomorrow afternoon—" He grinned. "I guess Keith won't be in much shape to fight. Anyway, Mr. Shinsura said you might be in some kind of trouble and asked me to round up some karate students and head over here. He mentioned something about some papers in a box."

"So, he finally decided to use Mr. Watanabe's clues," Frank said. "We're glad you guys were here—and on *our* side," said Frank. "Tanaka's 'ninjas' may not be the best fighters around, but there were too many of them and too few of us."

Joe just grinned. "I think Jim Lao will love this story when he hears it."

Paul turned to Tikko. "Hey," he said, with real admiration in his voice. "Where did you learn those moves?"

"From my uncle and father, of course!" She

laughed. "You might say karate is our family business."

A police officer came over to Frank and Joe, who were busy giving statements to Colonel Kelsey.

"Pardon me, Colonel. I have a message for the Hardys."

The boys looked at him curiosly. The officer patted his walkie-talkie. "I just had word from Detective Riley, at headquarters in Bayport," he said. "He wanted me to tell you that the grenade was traced to the armory at Redcliff—and that it has some prints on it. The lab will have a report tomorrow."

Joe and Frank grinned at each other. "Good old Con, always on the job," said Frank. "With the evidence here, that should be the icing on the cake!"

The next day Frank, Joe, and Tikko and her father decided to pay a call at the hospital. Along with the forces of the law, Fenton Hardy had brought them the welcome news that Mr. Watanabe had emerged from his coma and was asking to see his family.

When they arrived, the doctor even gave permission for everyone to visit at once, provided that they did not stay long.

Tikko peeked around the corner of the hospital-room door. "Uncle?" she called softly.

"Hello, my little star," her uncle replied. He was propped up in bed, looking tired but happy.

"My doctor tells me that I have caused you some excitement."

Tikko entered the room, followed by her father and the Hardys. "Oh, my—everyone! A party!" said the sensei, faintly smiling. "Are we celebrating?"

Mr. Shinsura spoke. "We are indeed, brother. We are celebrating the return of honor." The sensei looked alarmed, then disbelieving.

"You've solved our problem?" he asked.

"The Hardys and Tikko are the ones who really solved the problem for us—by refusing to run away from it."

Mr. Shinsura looked proudly at his daughter. Then, as they pulled up chairs, he began to relate the story of their adventures.

"Wait, Dad, please," Tikko said, laying a hand on his arm. Then she approached the side of the bed. "Uncle Seino, my father has stuck by his word to you. He has refused, even in the face of great danger, to tell me what was in the package you sent to him. He even refused to open it himself—until the seriousness of the criminal danger persuaded him he had no choice. Don't you think I deserve to know now?"

"Yes, Tikko, you do," said the sensei. "You may have deserved to know a long time ago." Mr. Watanabe pulled himself up a little more and began the story.

"Your mother was very ill for a long time before she died. Care for her condition was extremely expensive. When your father asked me to help, I knew of a way to make a great deal of money very fast—by teaching the art of karate to certain men."

He sighed. "I tried to ignore the fact that they would use my art with no sense of honor. But when I learned that the men I taught were Yakuza, I tried to end my agreement with them. They threatened you and your family, forcing me to sign a contract with them."

"Mr. Tanaka told us that much," said Tikko.

"Well, then. Before I left Tokyo—after they destroyed my house and everything I still held dear—I went to their headquarters in the night and stole my contract. It was the only proof that I had ever broken my solemn vow as a sensei. Perhaps I should have destroyed it—but I preferred to keep it, to remind me of my folly."

"But, Uncle Seino, it wasn't foolish to try to help your own sister! You loved her very much."

"I did love her, indeed. But I could—and should—have found another way to help her."

"I think I'm the one who was foolish," Mr. Shinsura said. "*I* should have gone to the Yakuza. After all, an electrical engineer, no matter how good, is not so rare as the perfect karate master. They would have learned to live without me."

"Well, it's all history now," said the sensei. "And before we forget—thank you, Joe and Frank. You've done us a great service. Frank—would you like to try for your black belt next year?"

Both Frank and Joe winced at the notion of any

more martial arts just then. "We'll see, sensei," Frank said, laughing. "I'll consider it when my bruises heal—if you can promise that neither of us will ever have to fight a ninja again."

"You've got a deal," said the sensei with a smile. "As soon as *my* bruises heal."